Perfect Convergence

Ruthless Desires 2

Elira Firethorn

Copyright © 2022 by Elira Firethorn

All rights reserved.

No portion of this book may be reproduced in any form without written permission from the publisher or author, except as permitted by U.S. copyright law.

To my little sister—
thanks for cheering me on.

Playlist & Storyboard

Playlist:

Lights Down Low - MAX, Garrett Nash

I GUESS I'M IN LOVE - Clinton Kane

Infinity (PRETTY YOUNG Remix) - Jaymes Young

Fallin' - AVAION, Why So Sad

There You Are - ZAYN

Church - Chase Atlantic

Die For You - The Weeknd

Smoke - Son Lux Remix - BOBI ANDONOV

Make Me Feel - Elvis Drew

Scars - Boy Epic

Walk Through Fire - Zayde Wølf, Ruelle

Man or a Monster (feat. Zayde Wølf) - Sam Tinnesz

Storyboard:

You can find Perfect Convergence's storyboard by going to pinterest.com/elirafirethorn.

Trigger Warning

Perfect Convergence is a dark romance book intended for people over the age of eighteen. It contains some sensitive content, including swearing, an implication of body shaming, violence, murder, a graphic description of a corpse, and a character having a panic attack. There are also fully detailed sex scenes, which include bondage, spitting, blood play, edging, semi-public sex (no one sees), and degradation. If you think any of those will affect you negatively, I recommend steering clear of this novella. There's no shame in it! Your mental health is more important. Please take care of yourselves, my friends.

Chapter One

Rhett

When I wake, I'm in an unfamiliar room, my hand resting in something wet and sticky.

I jerk awake. Where am I? How long have I been out?

A bit of light creeps underneath the closed door of the bedroom, and a light, sweet scent hits my nose that reminds me of the past weekend.

Wren. I fell asleep at Wren's place.

Reaching for the lamp, I turn it on and hold my fingers up to the light—then freeze. Why is there blood on the sheets?

I rip the blankets off my body and jump out of bed. We've made plenty of enemies. Would they come after her this quickly? Would they at all?

Fuck. What if they did? And while I was sleeping with her wrapped up in my arms, no less.

"Wren?" I call out. No answer. The clock says it's not even five yet.

Opening the door, I stalk down the hallway to where a soft light glows in the kitchen and living area.

"Wren, are you okay?" I scan the open space but come up empty.

No. *No.* We were supposed to be able to keep her safe.

I hear a small moan from the other side of the couch, on the . . . floor? What the hell?

Coming around, I find Wren on the area rug in something similar to a child's pose. But she has two throw pillows stacked up under her torso, and I can just barely make out a heating pad pressed to her lower stomach.

"Wren?" Crouching beside her, I place a hand gently on the small of her back.

She yelps, sitting up straight and narrowly missing my chin with the top of her head. When she sees me, she relaxes, pulling her earbuds out of her ears.

No wonder she couldn't hear me.

"Hi," she says, a little breathless. "I was trying not to wake you. Did the light bother you? Did I make too much noise?"

I shrug, pushing a few stray hairs out of her face. "I slept for a long time, considering. Are you okay? There's blood on the sheets."

She looks at my fingers and the blood staining them, then winces. "Sorry. It was probably gross to wake up to."

I frown. "More like worrisome. Did you hurt yourself?"

"Oh, no, I . . ." She looks down at the floor.

And then I realize that she's still pressing the heating pad to her stomach even though she's sitting up.

"Oh," I say at the same time she says, "I got my period in the middle of the night."

My shoulders sag with relief. "I thought you might be hurt."

"Hurt?" she laughs. "How would I have gotten hurt?"

I run a hand over my face. This isn't something I can explain. Maybe one day, but not now—or any time soon. "I dunno. Guess my mind just went there first because I haven't spent long periods of time around grown women."

And, come to think of it, I know embarrassingly little about women's menstrual cycles.

"Mmm." Wren adjusts herself so she's sitting on her ass with her back to the front of the couch. She leans her head back onto the seat cushions.

For a moment, I just stare at her. The graceful curve of her neck has my hands itching to trace the exposed skin. She's in a T-shirt and leggings with her hair tied up messily, but she still looks as beautiful as she did when I laid eyes on her at the masquerade ball the other night.

Our silence is broken by her phone going off.

"Shoot," Wren mutters, grabbing it. "That's my alarm. I have to get ready for work."

"But you look like you're in pain."

She gives me a smile that reminds me of the way a mother would look at a toddler who just asked an ignorant question. "Period cramps aren't really a valid excuse for taking off work. If you can walk, then you just have to deal. And I," she says with a grunt as she gets to her feet, wincing, "can walk."

"That's ridiculous. You can barely stand," I protest, watching as she clutches the heating pad to her until the cord pulls tight. She sighs, seeming to remember that she can't take it with her, before dropping it to the ground. Then she walks to the kitchen, bent over.

"There's coffee." She nods to the pot on the counter.

"Can you take pain meds?"

"Ran out." Opening the fridge, she stares inside for a minute before closing it again. When she turns around to face me, it really looks like the mere sight of food made her sick. "I'll be fine. The first day or two suck, but after that I can almost forget I'm on my period. To be honest, I'm lucky. Mine usually doesn't even last a whole week."

She hobbles down the hallway before disappearing into her bedroom. With a sigh, I rinse my fingers off and pour myself a mug—one of the few dishes her ex didn't break—of black coffee and take a few sips.

A couple minutes later, Wren comes back into the kitchen dressed in black skinny jeans and a black T-shirt. She's put on a bit of makeup, but it doesn't do much to hide the tiredness and pain on her face.

"I have to get going." She steps up to me, cupping my cheek with her hand before pressing a soft kiss to my lips. "Thank you for bringing me back last night."

"I'm driving you to work."

"It's only a couple of blocks. I usually walk."

"It's fucking freezing outside, Wren. And it snowed so much last night. The sidewalks won't be shoveled yet."

She bites her lip, considering my words. I'm about to tell her that if she decides to walk, I'll have no choice but to carry her, because she shouldn't even have to go into work when she's in this much pain. But she nods, giving me a small smile and another kiss.

"Thank you."

I down the rest of my coffee. As she ties on her boots, I grab my coat from where she tore it off me last night and then flip the heating pad off. By the time my own boots are on, she's ready—even though she looks like she needs to go back to bed.

She holds my hand on the elevator ride down, her head leaning against my shoulder. Elliot and Oliver never touch me this much. They know I need my personal space. But I can't find it in me to push Wren away.

Once we're in my truck, it only takes a minute for me to navigate the barely plowed streets. I pull up in front of the coffee shop, and Wren lets out a quiet sigh.

"Be careful of ice," I say, expecting her to turn and hop out of the truck. But instead, she turns to me, taking one of my hands in hers. They're freezing from the steering wheel, but she doesn't seem to mind.

Kissing my fingertips, she says, "I will. You sure it's safe to drive back to your house? The roads aren't great."

I have plenty of experience driving in the snow, so I nod. "Want me to text you when I get back?" It's something Elliot and I started doing when Oliver was at a particularly low point with his anxiety.

"That would be nice."

Leaning closer to her, I brush my lips against her cheek before kissing her. "You got it. Now get inside before you freeze."

With a smile that makes it feel much less cold out, she slides out of the truck just as Ava walks up to the front door. She pulls out a key, and they shuffle into the coffee shop.

Before I drive away, it doesn't go unnoticed by me that Ava is giving Wren a knowing look, and that Wren is staring bashfully at the floor. I chuckle. And then I'm off, knowing I need to make a couple of stops before I get home.

Chapter Two

Wren

"So?" Ava says, shooting me a look as we walk into the back and dump our stuff in the break room. "Tell me everything! How was your Valentine's Day night of debauchery? Oh, and who the hell dropped you off? I couldn't see through the windows."

"Actually," I say, grinning, "it was a whole *weekend* of debauchery. And I may have gotten three boyfriends out of it. Rhett dropped me off."

Ava's jaw drops. And then she's laughing, clutching her stomach as her face turns bright red from a lack of oxygen. "I KNEW IT! I *knew* they all liked you! Was it good? Was it *amazing?!* Oh my god, did they all go at you at once? Tell. me. everything."

I fill Ava in on as many details as I'm comfortable sharing, which isn't many, since I don't want to betray the guys' trust by blabbing about everything we did. Thankfully, she seems satisfied with what I decide to tell her.

We go through our opening routine smoothly. I move slower than normal, thanks to my cramps and stupid lack of painkillers. Maybe I can stop by the store on the way home and grab some.

A half hour after we clock in, there's a knock on the glass of the front door. Rolling my eyes, I head out to where some regular is probably waiting, thinking they can get their coffee early because they have a familiar face.

But my heart skips a beat when my eyes lock with Rhett's. My god. Will his calm, steady gaze ever *not* take my breath away?

I certainly hope not.

As I unlock the door, he gives me the faintest smile.

"Hey. Ummm. What are you doing here?"

He holds up a white plastic bag, and I can just make out a variety of pill bottles sitting at the bottom. "I wasn't sure what kind is best for period cramps, so I bought them all."

As I take the bag from him, warmth spreads through my chest. He got me pain meds? Has anyone ever done something this sweet for me? Maybe Ava, I suppose. "Rhett. You didn't have to."

"I didn't want you to be in pain all day."

If I could get away with dragging this man into the bathroom and kissing him—and maybe more—until he can barely stand, I would. But, unfortunately, I can't.

"Thank you."

"Anything," he says gently, a callback to what he told me last night.

I know this is all overwhelmingly fast for you, but I want to make this work. And last. So please—if I'm ever not giving you what you need from me, just tell me. I'll do anything to keep you, Wren.

I'm pretty sure I'm melting. But the warm fuzzies I'm feeling freeze over when a flicker of discomfort flashes across Rhett's face.

"I should go," he says, rubbing the back of his neck.

"Right. Yeah. Um, thank you. Really, you just made my day a lot less miserable." I reach out and squeeze his hand.

He relaxes a little. Then, with a quick kiss on my forehead, he leaves.

"What a sweetheart," Ava says with a sigh, pressing her hands over her heart. "He's officially forgiven for not laughing at my joke a couple weeks ago."

I snort.

"What? It was a good joke!"

I open one of the bottles and wash two pills down with some water. Then I smirk. "It was all right. I *guess*."

She swats at me, and I laugh. And then we're back to work, getting everything prepared for our first morning rush.

...

Despite the painkillers, my shift still sucks. When I'm finally done and grab my stuff from the back, I scroll through my notifications on my phone. Rhett texted me when he got home, which was really sweet. Unfortunately, in the early afternoon, my mom called me multiple times and left me with a wall of texts.

Mom: We need to talk.

Mom: I just spoke with Adam's mom. What's going on?!

Mom: Young lady, answer me!

Mom: You're messing everything up. Wren, you're meant to be with Adam. You're perfect for each other. What happened to the family you were going to start? You can't make babies forever, you know. Clock's ticking.

I cringe. There she goes again with her traditionalist bullshit. If that's what a woman wants, then fine. After dating Adam for a while, I thought it *was* what I wanted—he always told me he was going to be the provider for me and the family we were planning on having eventually.

Funny, considering he *wasn't*. We both had to work our asses off to make rent.

I sigh. As if I needed another reminder that I either have to get a new roommate or find a cheaper apartment. Or a better job. My savings will only last for a few months.

"Let's just get this over with," I grumble. After wishing Ava a quick goodbye, I start the walk home. Thankfully, the sidewalks are shoveled.

My mom answers her phone on the second ring. "Wren! Finally! Why have you been ignoring me?"

"I've been at work."

Of course, she wouldn't understand that. She hasn't had a job—besides raising me—since before I was born.

"Well, whatever. Maybe if we talked more often, I would be able to remember your schedule."

I roll my eyes. It's been the same for almost two years—first shift, Monday through Friday. "What do you need?"

"What do I need? Are you kidding me? Your boyfriend was in the *hospital* over the weekend, and Mary Anne says you didn't even visit him."

"He's not my boyfriend."

"Wh-*excuse* me?"

"He's not my boyfriend, mom."

"Last I checked he was!"

"Well, I broke up with him. A while ago." *I just didn't tell you because I didn't want to deal with you freaking out on me.*

Of course, my mother doesn't even ask why I ended our years-long relationship. Doesn't even assume that maybe Adam was the problem. Instead, she launches into a rant I've heard a thousand times over the years whenever one of my "rebellious" cousins is brought up.

I barely listen, focusing more on avoiding people on the sidewalk and watching out for patches of ice. At least the sun is out, which helps to counteract the bitter cold biting at my skin.

"Adam was going to give you everything you've ever dreamed of. Everything a woman could want! Financial stability, a loving husband and father of your children. What more could you ask for?"

I grimace. *Loving?* Once upon a time, I would've called Adam that. If we were still together, I probably still would be. But now? Now that we're broken up, all I can see are the ugly parts of him.

The parts that made me feel unwanted. Annoying. Like he was bored with me, only staying with me out of obligation. I was never good enough, never submissive enough, never like his friends' girlfriends.

"He was going to propose, you know. And you didn't even visit him in the hospital. How could you be so cruel?"

"He was going to *what?*" I screech so loudly that I get a few surprised glances from people walking past.

He was going to propose? While he was actively cheating on me?!

I'd tell my mother that, but I know her well enough to be able to predict how that will go. Either she'll tell me it was my fault, or she won't believe me.

Best to avoid that trainwreck.

"You broke that poor boy's heart. And then he got jumped in his own home! Can you believe it?"

"He . . . what?" My voice is too high. I ball my free hand into a fist. There's no way I can let on that I know what happened to Adam—or, more specifically, *who* happened.

"That's right! He could've died." My mom sighs. "I thought this is what you wanted, Wren. Adam is on track to be a very successful young man. What happened to your future together?"

I hesitate. *Is* that what I want? Before I met Adam, I had a plan—a dream. It was silly, maybe a little naïve, but it was mine.

All I wanted was to become a freelance graphic designer, learn a lot of languages, and travel the world. I figured that if I could work from anywhere, I could stay in lots of different countries, learn their languages, and experience their cultures.

I could spend time outside hiking and exploring. I could learn lots of cool new words. Discover new ways to cook. Listen to people tell their history, their stories. So much *learning*. And I thought that maybe I could make a living designing things like book covers and logos and social media graphics and—

I stop dead in my tracks. Where the hell did that dream go? Why did I ever stop pursuing it?

You know why, I tell myself. *You're just too ashamed of yourself to admit it.*

"Wren? Wren, are you still there? Hellooooo?"

I hang up, ignoring my phone vibrating in my pocket when she tries to call me back. The last thing I need right now is my mother lecturing me.

When I get home, I drop my bag and coat on the floor. After stripping, I step into the shower. The hot water warms my frozen skin, and I imagine it washing away my mother's words, too.

It doesn't work.

And all I'm left with is the cold, bitter realization that I've lost myself, and that the past years I've spent with Adam have all been one gigantic, messy waste.

Chapter Three

Oliver

Warmth.

That's what I wake up to. Warmth, a big arm draped over me, and the beginnings of morning light streaming through the windows of Elliot's room.

There's also a very familiar, very hard *something* pressing into my ass.

Ell groans behind me, his arm tightening around my waist. Slowly, I turn around and nuzzle my face in his neck. Then I inhale deeply, taking in his scent, all sandalwood and citrus and him.

"I love waking up with you," he mumbles sleepily.

I smile against his skin. "Why, because I always let you fuck me in the morning?"

He chuckles, squeezing my side and kissing the top of my head. "That's nice, too."

His cock twitches against my leg, and I wrap my hand around it.

"Fuck," Elliot groans.

I grin, pulling my head away from him to watch his face. He's opened his eyes, and they're filled with want.

Perfect. I want to keep his mind occupied a while longer before he remembers what happened last night.

I stayed with him, showering with him and listening as he voiced his worries and paced the bedroom. But there was only so much I could do to help him through the guilt of hurting Wren. Hell, there's really *nothing* I can do, except give him a good distraction.

Elliot lets me stroke him for a minute before he's thrusting into my hand, moaning and fisting the sheets. Then he grunts, "Get on your hands and knees, O."

I oblige with a grin. He's on me in seconds, ripping off my boxers and spreading my cheeks. Then I feel him licking the area around my hole, and I groan.

"You want more, do you?" he mumbles.

"Do you even have to ask?"

"Want my cock pounding into you, I bet."

I groan. *Fuck yes.*

He squeezes one of my ass cheeks, finally licking my hole. His tongue moves in a pattern that has me biting my lip to keep from begging for more. When he pulls away, I moan in protest.

"One second." He crawls over the blankets to his nightstand, where he pulls out a tube of lube. Then he smirks at the desperate look on my face.

God, I love seeing him like this, completely naked and towering over me. Confident. Dominant. Perfectly . . . *Elliot.*

"Are you going to fuck me," I say, "or just keep staring at me?"

He shrugs. "I could look at you like this all day, on your hands and knees, all needy for me."

"Really? With your hands off?"

He runs his tongue over his teeth before he grins. "Yeah, definitely not." And then he's behind me again, his tongue working its magic for another minute. "Ready for more?"

"You know I am."

He prods into me with a lubed-up finger, moving in and out gently. When he adds a second finger, I move my hips back to meet his hand.

"Someone's impatient." The pleased satisfaction in Elliot's voice has me even more desperate for him.

When he inserts a third finger, he stops moving, letting me fuck myself on them instead. Finally, after I'm ready to explode from anticipation, he pulls out.

"Edge of the bed on your back."

I scramble to follow his instructions, bringing my knees to my chest once I'm laying down. He slips off the bed, coating his cock with lube as he walks over to me.

"Ready?"

"God yes."

He lines himself up, pushing into me with a dark, satisfied rumble sounding from his throat. He stays gentle at first, letting me adjust, but I know it won't last.

By far, Rhett is the kinkiest of us. But Elliot has his rough side, too. Even I do, although I enjoy being on the receiving end more.

As Elliot picks up his pace, we both groan. Then he wraps his clean hand around my dick, stroking me as he slams into me.

Part of me is surprised—and a little disappointed—that Elliot didn't take the time to tie me up or restrain me in some way. But the look in his eyes tells me he's just as impatient as I am.

"You feel so fucking good, Ell," I grit out.

"Damn right I do." He thrusts into me.

I moan, closing my eyes. He doesn't let up, with his cock or with his hand, and within minutes his confidence is driving me maddeningly close to finishing. Of course, it's not *just* his confidence. It's that he's had years upon years to explore my body, and he hasn't left a single inch unturned.

Elliot is well acquainted with the many ways to fuck me into oblivion, and he knows it.

"You're going to make me come," I pant.

He smirks, somehow managing to fuck me even harder. "That's right. And it's going to push me over the edge. And then you're going to take every last drop of cum I give you. Understood?"

"Fuck. Yes. *Yes.*"

It doesn't even take another minute before I let out a yell and come all over my stomach. Elliot must've been trying to hold himself back, because within seconds, he's groaning, his thrusts finally slowing as he comes inside me.

Swearing, Elliot pants, "I love the way you feel."

With a grin, I sit up. He plants a kiss on my forehead as he pulls out. We're both hot and sweaty, and my stomach is a sticky mess, but I don't care. This weekend was amazing, and this feels like a blissful extension of it.

"I love *you*, Ell."

"Mmm. And I love you."

"How could you not? I'm practically perfect." I wink at him.

He rolls his eyes. "Let's get cleaned up."

Chapter Four

Rhett

At home, I find Oliver and Elliot curled up in Ell's bed, still sound asleep. By the time I go on a run and take a quick shower, I can hear them just starting to get up.

So I head downstairs in nothing but a pair of shorts and get some coffee brewing. By the time I have it poured and breakfast almost done, they're shuffling into the kitchen, hair still damp from their shower.

Oliver grins when he sees me. "Omelettes? You're the best. I'm keeping you."

I snort. "Like you could ever get rid of me."

Yawning, Oliver wraps his arms around me from behind. He presses his face into the bare skin of my back, and his words vibrate down my spine. "Wouldn't want to."

My skin crawls, but my chest warms with satisfaction. "I know."

"How was Wren this morning?"

Elliot pauses after Oliver asks the question, his coffee mug halfway to his mouth. That look of guilt travels across his face for a few seconds before he takes a sip.

"Tired," I say. "But happy, I think."

I hesitate to reveal more. Elliot, Oliver, and I have been pretty open with each other when it comes to what we've learned about Wren, unless it's something more personal that she might like to reveal to each of us separately.

But I have no idea what proper period etiquette is.

My sister was killed when she was a child. And when it came to things like periods and sex, my mother was fairly squeamish.

Do I tell them Wren's on her period? Do I not? Does it matter? What if she doesn't care if people know she's on her period, and I'm being weird? What if she *does* care?

I think it's probably best I keep my mouth shut.

"You sleep well?" Elliot's voice is quiet, and he won't look at anything but his coffee.

"Yeah." I shove a plate in front of where he's sitting at the counter. "Really well, actually."

"Good."

By the time I've made Oliver's omelette and my own, Elliot has barely picked at his. Oliver is watching him with concern. Omelettes are Elliot's favorite.

"She seems okay, you know." I watch him closely.

Elliot sets his fork down before resting his face in his hands. "It doesn't matter. I can't take back that I said it was best for us to forget her."

"Elliot." I round the counter, grabbing his shoulder and turning him on the stool until he's facing me. "Mistakes are a part of being human."

It's a hard truth I've become intimately familiar with over the past few years. One that Ell and Oliver have to remind me of constantly.

He leans his forehead against my chest. "I wish I never said it."

Oliver runs a hand down his back. "You were trying to protect her, Ell. Being reasonable is what you do best. Hell, it's the only reason the three of us are still alive."

It's true. Oliver and I tend to be more impulsive. Elliot's patience and reasoning have saved us from running blindly into quite a few bad situations that would've gotten us killed otherwise.

"I still hurt her. You guys saw her face."

"Yeah, I did," Oliver says. "But I also saw her face when she was saying goodbye to you last night. Wanna know how she looked then?"

Elliot sighs and shakes his head.

"Like she'd worship the ground you walked on if you let her. She gets it, Ell. Even though she doesn't have the whole picture. I don't think she's holding a grudge at all."

Blowing out a breath, Elliot says, "We'll see."

The discomfort on his face is one I'm all too familiar with. "Have we gotten anywhere with the Williams job?" Hopefully, a subject change will give Elliot some relief.

He nods. "Just the first round of the usual stuff. Address, family, finances, security. His home is practically a fortress, so we're going to have to get him in public. He also has two bodyguards with him at all times."

Already, I can see the guilt fading from Elliot's eyes, replaced by determination. His entire demeanor lightens as he outlines his ideas to tail Williams and set up a spot to ambush him.

This is his favorite part—the researching, the planning. It's like putting a puzzle together without knowing where all the pieces are. For most people, it'd be frustrating. But Elliot? He loves the challenge.

And the Williams job seems particularly challenging. Good. Sometimes distraction is the best solution—temporarily, at least.

Edgar Williams is some of our city's top scum. A successful businessman known for cutting corners, having a short temper, and exploiting his workers—in and out of the States.

On more than one occasion, I've contemplated taking him out myself. Getting hired to do it should sweeten the deal.

But it only leaves a bitter taste in my mouth. There's a possibility it has something to do with a beautiful, smart woman who very well might hightail it out of this relationship the second she realizes what we do.

She knows that being with us might put her in danger. But I don't think she *really* understands what that means. And that's no one's fault but our own. Because we thought we'd never be able to have her, and now? Now that we have a chance, none of us are willing to let it go.

Which, unfortunately, means letting things go unexplained.

"We're going to tell Wren eventually, right?"

Oliver and Elliot stare at me. It takes a second for me to realize that I interrupted Ell while he was in the middle of explaining what we're going to do today and tomorrow.

"I don't like keeping her in the dark," Oliver says.

"Neither do I." Sighing, Elliot cuts into his omelette with his fork. "But it's a lot to spring on someone."

"Is there a way to ease her into it?" As Oliver says it, he glances between me and Ell, but the look in his eyes tells me that he already knows the answer.

How do you ease a woman into telling her that the three men she's in a relationship with are killers? You don't. Either you hide it and hope to get away with it, or you tell her and hope for the best.

And the longer you keep it from her, the less the odds are in your favor.

"I don't want to break her trust," Elliot says. "Not again."

"I mean. We refused to tell her what we do. So she knows we're hiding something."

"Yeah, but why would her mind go to us being hitmen?"

PERFECT CONVERGENCE

Oliver palms the back of his neck. "Fuck, how mad do you think she'll be?"

My stomach sinks at his question and the silent admission that there's no chance she could accept it *without* getting upset.

With a groan, Elliot rubs his face. "We need to stay focused on the job. We have exactly a week to kill him. After that, we'll figure out how and when to explain everything to Wren."

Right. Taking out Edgar Williams is our priority right now.

"So we spend today and tomorrow learning more about his security team?" I'm pretty sure that's what Elliot said while I was lost in thought.

"Yeah. Supposedly, he's meeting a business partner at Garden Grille tomorrow evening."

A restaurant downtown—owned by Williams, of course.

"You think that'll be our best shot?" Oliver asks.

Elliot shrugs. "It's the only time I know he'll be away from his house. I have Finn trying to get us more intel, but he has to be careful who he talks to. The last thing we want to do is tip Williams off."

I frown. That'll be tough. Taking a man down in a public place comes with a lot of problems, including traumatizing everyone who happens to be there at the time. His murder is supposed to be high profile, but not like that.

"We hit him on his way home?"

Elliot stays quiet. As we watch, he squints his eyes ever so slightly, a sign that he's taking in all the puzzle pieces he has. Comparing them to each other, seeing which ones fit where, figuring out what he still needs.

I'd be lying if I said I didn't find it hot as hell.

After a few minutes, he says, "We only have one shot at this. If we don't kill him the first time around, he'll go into hiding. We could probably get into his house, but I don't want to take that risk."

Neither Oliver nor I need to ask what risk he's talking about. It's the one we've decided never to take, no matter how well a job pays. There's no amount of cash that could make losing one of us worth it.

It's not that we don't take dangerous jobs. We do. But we're always able to outsmart the system. Keep ourselves hidden. Avoid the impossible situations.

Usually, that is. When we were only in this to get revenge on the man who killed my little sister, things were different. We were young. Angry.

It took almost losing Oliver for us to realize that we needed to re-prioritize. Us first, and then revenge.

I guess that's how we got started in all this. We had to acquire certain skills to take down the crime lord who killed Sammy.

In the meantime, we've become the guys you go to when you need someone dead. We have the means and the know-how, so it was basically a natural progression.

"We tail him all night. We'll have to take different cars and switch on and off so no one notices us following him. The Garden Grille has enough windows that we won't have to go inside to monitor him. If an opportunity presents itself, we take him out. Otherwise, once he makes a move to head home, two of us will get ahead and cut him off on his road. The third will follow Williams from far enough behind and act as backup in case we need help."

He goes on, giving more details of his plan, shoving food into his mouth in between sentences. As he does, my confidence builds. We've definitely handled worse before.

By the time he's done talking, we've all finished eating. Almost immediately, the guilt is back in Ell's eyes.

Oliver nudges him. "She'll be okay."

Elliot says nothing for a minute. Last night, when Wren overheard him, he immediately knew he'd made a mistake.

But what he can't seem to grasp is that Wren understands why he said it. It was to protect her, to shield her from the potential danger and pain that could be a result of her entering into a relationship with us.

Wren seemed to get it last night. But Elliot *hasn't*.

"I think I'm gonna see what else I can find on Williams." Elliot rinses off his plate, then sets it in the sink. "Dive a little deeper. You know."

Translation: I'm going to sit in my office and feel like shit all day.

Oliver and I exchange a glance. Then he gives me a mischievous grin.

"Don't worry," he murmurs. "I know exactly how to fix this."

Chapter Five

Elliot

I spend the morning and afternoon locked in my office, gathering every morsel of information I can find on Williams' security team.

All except one are your standard ex-military guys who've gone into private security. The other? Tyler Williams, Edgar's nephew and right-hand man. Rumor has it that Edgar is grooming him to take over his empire one day.

But that's not what I care about. It's the fact that he's wildly reckless, but it always works out for him. Stick him in a dangerous situation in which he's not in control, and he'll gain it quickly—usually leaving a trail of bodies in his wake.

We're planning an ambush, which gives us the element of surprise. But if Tyler is going to be with Edgar tomorrow night, that might still put them at an advantage. He's clever, unpredictable, and fast.

We'll have to be careful.

Sometime in the late afternoon, there's a knock on my door. Oliver slips inside, followed by Rhett. Both are giving me a look that says my time of moping alone is over.

I sit back in my chair, watching both of them in silence. Rhett leans against the doorframe, arms crossed over his chest, while Oliver walks right up to my desk.

"What do we do when we need to fix something, Elliot?"

I chew on my lip for a second. There's no way I'm going to like where this conversation is going. "Ignore it?"

"*Ell.*"

It's the wrong answer, and I know it. It's also distinctly unlike me to avoid my problems. But I can't get it out of my head that at any moment, Wren is going to text me and tell me that she has no desire to be with someone who was willing to toss her aside so easily.

Not that it was an easy decision. In fact, I'm ridiculously grateful Wren fought against it and changed my mind.

"What do we do, Ell?" Rhett says. His gaze is calm. Cool. Authoritative. This man isn't in the mood to take anyone's shit.

Who am I kidding? He never is.

"We fix the goddamned problem," I grumble.

Oliver grins, and the sparkle in his eyes tells me he has something up his sleeve. "That's right. Now get up. We're going for a ride."

. . .

"I don't like this."

I'm in Rhett's truck, arms crossed, glaring at him and Oliver from the backseat. If I'd known *go for a drive* actually meant *head to Wren's place*, I never would've agreed to this.

No idea what else they could've meant, though.

I eye Wren's apartment building warily. "There's no way I'm just going up there unannounced. What if she's busy?"

Oliver chuckles. "Oh, she knows you're coming."

"What?" I snap. Then I narrow my eyes.

"No backing out now, Ell. Get your ass up there. Text us when you're ready to come home."

Rhett gives me a *don't you dare protest* look in the rearview mirror.

I swallow. "She knows I'm coming?"

They both nod.

I'm so fucked.

I hop out of the truck, shoving my hands into my coat pockets. The whole way up to her floor, my mind is a whirlwind of anxiety.

Did Wren ask the guys to bring me here? Is she going to tell me she wants nothing to do with me?

You'd deserve it if she did.

The thought makes my heart ache. Minus the months of silently pining after her and doing my best to make meaningful conversation at the coffee shop, she's only been in my life for three days. Yet it feels like it's been so much longer.

There's something about the way she fits with us that's just... *right*. It's the same way I've always felt about Oliver and Rhett.

I wipe my sweaty palms on my jeans before knocking on Wren's door. Within seconds, it's swinging open, and I'm looking down at the woman who none of us can seem to get enough of.

... Except the energy and sass that sparked in her eyes all weekend is gone, replaced by exhaustion.

Still, she perks up slightly when she meets my gaze, and it eases the tension in my chest some.

"Elliot." She pulls me into a hug, kissing my cheek as she does.

"Hi." The word comes out too tense.

When she pulls away, she strokes my cheek, frowning. "You don't look too good. Do you need to sit down? Or maybe drink some water?"

I need to not lose you.

"I'm okay." Then I look her up and down. "I mean this in the kindest way possible, but you don't look too good, either."

She laughs, turning and heading further into her apartment. "At least I have an excuse."

Fuck. *Fuck.* Am I the reason?

"I'm sorry," I blurt, stepping in and shutting the door behind me. "I . . . Things shouldn't've—uh. I never should've said what I said. Never should've thought it."

Jesus Christ. Where are all the communication skills I've learned over the past twenty-eight years of my life? Gone, apparently.

She turns, giving me a quizzical look. "What?"

"I didn't want to make you miserable."

She brings a hand up to her mouth to stifle a giggle. "Elliot. This isn't because of what happened yesterday evening."

"Oh." I breathe a sigh of relief.

"I guess I figured Rhett would've told you. I got my period last night, and the first couple days are always miserable."

Ah. So that's why Rhett was acting awkward this morning when Oliver asked how she was doing.

"*And* I talked to my mom after work," Wren continues, "which was terrible. She harassed me about Adam and told me I made a huge mistake by breaking up with him, and then she went on about how I need to start popping out babies, and it made me realize that I let Adam tell me how to live my life instead of sticking with my original plans, which were really fucking cool, actually, and now I'm just pissed at myself, and I don't even know if I *want* kids anymore, or any of the stuff I decided I wanted because I was with Adam, and—" Her eyes widen, and she stops.

I raise an eyebrow, waiting for her to go on, but she buries her face in her hands.

"Why do I keep dumping all of my shit on you?" she groans.

I step closer to her, but then I pause.

What if she doesn't want you to touch her?

"I don't mind listening," I say gently. "It sounds like you have a lot on your mind."

Friday night, she did something similar, talking about how Adam made her feel like she didn't matter to him. It broke my heart then—the thought of her not feeling like she was enough. And now? Well, I'm ready to follow in Rhett's footsteps and pay Adam another visit.

"I don't really want to think about it right now," Wren says. She wraps her arms around herself, rocking back on her heels. "Um. Did you eat dinner?"

"You don't have to make me anything."

"Oh, trust me, the last thing I want to do right now is cook." She moves through her tiny kitchen, opening a cupboard door. "My dinner plans include eating a shit ton of pretzels, cheese, and . . ." She turns, surveying her counters before grabbing a lone apple. "This!"

I smile but don't say anything, shoving my hands in my pockets. God, why do I feel so awkward right now?

Wren's smile fades as she takes me in. Then she sighs and sets down the apple, rounding the counter until we're only a few feet apart. For a minute, we just watch each other silently. She looks as uncomfortable as I feel.

"Wren . . ."

What am I even supposed to say? How do I make up for last night? I barely got a chance to apologize. And I can't imagine how I made Wren feel. Unwanted? Like I'm going to toss her aside at any moment? Like she's not worthy of keeping?

I don't know you that well, Wren. But I want to. And I want to keep you. I want to be in your life. I'm so sorry.

"It's okay to be scared." Her voice comes out soft and comforting as she steps into my reach. Her fingers fumble with the buttons of my coat before she has them all undone. Then she slips it off my shoulders and sets it on the back of her couch.

Biting the inside of my cheek, I watch her movements. Being scared isn't something I like admitting to. I'd rather be seen as the strong one. The one who can handle anything. Even though I know I can't.

"I'm scared too," she says quietly, stepping up to me. Her arms come around me, and she rests her head on my chest. "And not just because of last night. I'm scared I'll..." She pauses, sighing. "It doesn't matter right now. What *does* is that I understand you're scared. And it's okay."

My heart clenches in my chest. Knowing there's something bugging Wren, but not knowing what it is, or how to fix it, doesn't sit right with me. But I don't want to force her into talking about it if she's not ready.

"I don't want to hurt you," I murmur, pressing my lips to the top of her head for a brief moment. "It's why I said what I said. I know it doesn't make sense to you, I know it's probably frustrating that we're not telling you everything, but—"

"I know enough. And I understand, Elliot."

"Wren—"

"Call me love," she whispers, looking up at me. One of her hands leaves my waist so she can run her fingers along my jawbone.

"Love." I touch my forehead to hers, watching as she closes her eyes, a small smile dancing on her lips.

Relief floods my body at the content look on Wren's face. I have no idea how she can be so understanding when she has such little information. Although she's a smart woman. Maybe she's put together more than I'm giving her credit for.

Still, nervousness creeps back in. I don't like keeping things from her.

"Are you really okay with this? With not knowing? I don't want to make you anxious. And I don't want you to feel left out."

She opens her eyes to stare into mine. "Do you remember what you asked me our first night together?" Then she laughs to herself. "I suppose you asked me a lot of things. Do you remember when you asked if I trusted the three of you?"

"Of course."

Looking away, she takes a second to collect herself before saying, "I know it's probably silly. Maybe a little stupid. But I meant what I said, Elliot. I trust you. Do I have questions? Of course. Am I curious? Ridiculously. But you wanted to let me go for my own safety. And if you think you need to keep me in the dark about what you guys do for the same reason, then I can accept that. Not for forever, but for now, I can."

"It doesn't scare you? Not knowing?"

"Will you let anything happen to me?" As she asks, her gaze meets mine again, inquisitive. Her head tilts to the side ever so slightly.

"Never. We protect each other. And you're included in that now."

She hums softly, leaning her head against my shoulder. "It doesn't sound like I have anything to be afraid of, then."

I breathe deeply for the first time all day. How can she place that much trust in us so easily after only a weekend together? We did everything to make sure she was comfortable and felt safe, but this—this is a whole other level.

It makes me want to protect her even more than before.

"Do you think I'm being stupid?" she asks.

Holding her close, I kiss her temple. "Not at all."

With a little sigh, she relaxes into me, and the gesture tugs on my heartstrings. It's a similar sensation to how I felt when I realized I was falling for Oliver and Rhett.

With one hand still holding her close, I tilt her face up with two fingers under her chin. "May I kiss you?"

She beams up at me. "Yes."

Gently, I press my lips to hers. She rises to her tiptoes, wrapping her arms around my neck. The kiss stays slow, almost exploratory, and it soothes the anxiety that's been eating at me all day.

Then Wren tenses, and she pulls away, her head dropping to my chest with a grunt.

And just like that, the panic is back. "What's wrong?"

"Cramps," she groans. Her fingers curl into the fabric of my T-shirt. "They let up after the first few days, but until then, I . . ." She grimaces. "My pain meds must've worn off. I haven't been paying attention to the time."

Leading her to the couch, I help her sit. "Where are they?"

"Counter. They're in a shopping bag. Blue bottle."

I grab some, then search for a glass, only to come up empty.

Right. Adam destroyed most of her dishes.

I clean one of the two remaining mugs that are sitting in the sink before filling it with water. Then, grabbing the pill bottle, I bring them over to her.

"Is there anything else you do to help with the cramps?" I crouch by her legs, placing a hand on her thigh.

"Heating pad," she mumbles, swallowing two pills with a gulp of water. "Ice cream—well, that doesn't *actually* help. But it's nice. And, uh . . ." Biting her lip, she stares into her mug. Then she tugs on her hair nervously. "My god, Ava is right. I *am* hopeless."

"What?"

"I just—I get awkward a lot, when it comes to, like, flirting and . . . stuff." She lets out a half laugh. "Actually, I'm just awkward in general."

With a chuckle, I say, "I hadn't noticed."

She balks. "Really?!"

"I'm *joking,* love." Leaning down, I press a kiss to her thigh. They're bare, considering she's in shorts and a long-sleeved T-shirt.

"Oh. Right. Of course."

For a moment, I watch her squirm. Then I smile. *Flirting and stuff, huh?* "If you're trying to tell me that orgasms can help relieve period cramps, I happen to already know that."

Her eyes widen. Then she averts her gaze again and gulps down some more water. "How are you so goddamned perceptive?" she squeaks out.

She made a similar comment about my perceptiveness at the masquerade ball. My answer now is the same as it was then, although I don't dare say it out loud.

I've learned to read you because I can't take my eyes off of you whenever you're around.

"Maybe you're easy to read." I shrug. Then I take the mug from her hands and place it on the end table. "Do you want my help?" Again, I kiss her thigh. It's like I can barely resist her.

"With having an orgasm?"

"*Orgasms.* You'll be getting more than one if I have anything to say about it."

She bites her lip, and a look of uneasiness crosses her face.

My hand slides off her leg. "Only if you want, Wren."

"No, I do, I promise. I just . . ." She fiddles with the hem of her shirt. "I can't have, like, *actual sex*. It'll hurt too much."

"From your period? Or from the weekend?"

"Both," she says, staring bashfully at my shoulder. "Well, and Rhett may have fucked the hell out of me last night."

With a chuckle, I cup her chin and turn her head so she's looking at me. God, I love her eyes. "He's good at it, isn't he?"

She nods, smiling. Then that look of hesitation is on her face again.

"I have no plans to fuck you, Wren. I just want to help you feel better."

Her hands ball into fists. "I don't . . . you—I don't want you to feel like you have to do anything. It's just cramps. The pain meds will kick in soon enough anyway."

"Wren. It'd be my pleasure." As I say it, I trace my fingers down her arm, watching as her eyes flutter closed for a moment. Her legs open a few inches, and I'm not quite sure she did it consciously. "Did I not make it clear this weekend how much I love the way you taste?"

That seems to get her to relax some, because she laughs. "Trust me, it was *very* clear. But I don't want you to feel like you have to. You know, if periods gross you out."

"Not at all." *And I can think of someone who'd very much enjoy getting your blood all over himself.*

Some of the tension leaves Wren's shoulders as she takes a deep breath. "Okay. Then . . . then yes." She leans forward, her arms sliding around my neck, and kisses me.

I groan at the feeling of her lips on mine. Her movements become more desperate, her fingers curling into my hair.

She still wants you.

Fuck, what a relief.

She breathes in a tiny gasp when I push her shorts aside, tracing a finger up her panties. I do it again, and her legs part even more.

"Do you want me to take them off?" I ask, kissing up her thigh until my lips meet the edge of her underwear.

She nods, and then she's tugging them down her legs and tossing them to the floor. I groan at the sight of her, spreading her legs and tugging her to the edge of the couch cushion. Then I frown.

"No tampon? *And* no blood?"

"Menstrual cup." Her voice is breathy and light. "More convenient. And cheaper."

"Ah." I part her lips with my tongue, smiling to myself at the way she whimpers. Gently, I work her clit, not sure if she's sore there.

Slumping into the cushions, she swears under her breath. Then she's tugging on her hair again, moaning as I swirl my tongue.

Fuck, she's perfect like this.

"You're irresistible," I mutter into her skin, watching her eyes roll into the back of her head in response.

I wish I had something to tie her hands up with, since she doesn't seem to know what to do with them. But, of course, there are other ways to keep them occupied.

After a long, slow lick, I pull away. She whines in protest, her eyes popping open and meeting mine.

"Play with your nipples through your shirt. And don't stop until I say you can."

"As long as you don't stop, either. Please."

I raise an eyebrow. "You think you're in a position to make negotiations?"

With a grin, she says, "Since you've made it crystal clear you want this, yes." Her fingers brush over her pebbled nipples once, twice, three times.

What can I say? She's right. "You've got yourself a deal."

When I dive back in, I suck her clit into my mouth. She moans, her back arching off the couch as she continues to touch her nipples.

"Oh my god, Elliot. Please—just like that. Just like that."

I keep going, snaking an arm under her leg to hold her better. When I add my tongue, it takes a few minutes, and then she starts trembling.

That's it, love. Come for me. Be a good girl and let go.

I'd say it out loud, but the desperate sounds coming out of her mouth are too addictive for me to stop. Instead, I trace a finger around her entrance gently, not pushing inside, just teasing.

"Oh my god. *Ohmygod*, Elliot." She squirms against me, but I just hold her tighter. Then she claps a hand over her mouth as she cries out.

For another second, I don't change a thing. But when she tries to wiggle away, her body thrashing, I let up, giving her gentle licks as she rides out her climax and then comes back down to earth.

Her hands drop to her sides as I straighten. "Wow," she pants. Then her stomach growls, and she giggles.

I grab her clothes and slide them back up her legs. "Where's your heating pad?"

"Uh. Floor, I think." She peers over the side of the couch, and I follow her gaze.

Thankfully, the cord is long enough. I flip it on and place it over her lower stomach. "I'm going to get your dinner ready." I kiss her on her forehead, and when I pull away, she's watching me with a wide-eyed, soft gaze.

There are so many emotions in her expression. Trust, adoration, gratitude. It sucks me in until I'm pressing my lips to hers, savoring her tiny moans and the way she grabs my arms.

I break off the kiss, and she moves to get up. "Relax," I murmur, cupping her cheek. "Let me take care of you."

With a sigh, she settles into the couch, hugging the heating pad to her stomach. Then her eyes close, and I watch her for a split second longer before moving over to her tiny kitchen.

I think, I realize as I rummage around for a knife and cutting board, *I'd do just about anything to see that look on her face again.*

Chapter Six

Wren

At first, I was a little disappointed that I only got one orgasm when Elliot promised me multiple. But then he came back to the couch with a plate full of pretzels, cheese, and apple slices, and I swear I melted.

But that's not even the best part.

No, the best part is that he has me on his lap while he feeds me.

Is it possible to fall in love in four days? Because I think I might be doing just that.

Elliot holds the last apple slice up to my lips, and I bite into it, taking half. He pops the rest into his mouth, trailing his fingers down my spine.

Settling against him, I inhale his sandalwood and citrus scent. "You always smell so good."

He replies with a chuckle and a kiss on my forehead. "You full?"

"Yeah. Thank you."

"Of course," he murmurs. Then he stands, cradling me to his chest and carrying me through the apartment.

"What are you doing?"

"I believe I promised you multiple orgasms, did I not?"

There isn't a single thing that can stop the smile spreading over my face. "I was wondering about that."

In my room, he sets me on the bed. "Clothes off, then get on your knees."

I shiver, following his commands without a second thought. Once I'm in position, he takes me in with a satisfied expression. Then he crawls onto the bed and kisses me, his hands cradling my face.

Slipping my fingers under his shirt, I tug it up until he pulls it over his head. Before I even realize what I'm doing, my lips are on his hot skin, pressing kisses to his tattoos. I linger over the butterfly on his ribcage for a second, remembering our conversation the other night about Rhett's little sister.

She meant the world to all of us.

"Wren," he groans as my lips trail down his stomach. He pulls me up. "Don't distract me."

Before I can protest, he's lowered himself onto the mattress. He flips over onto his back, tugging me forward a bit. Then his hands are on my hips, forcing me to lower myself onto his face.

He groans, pressing a kiss to my clit before sucking on it. I cry out, falling forward but managing to catch myself. My hands fist the blankets as his tongue caresses me lightly, gently.

"Elliot," I pant. "More. Please."

With a low laugh that vibrates through me, he adds more pressure, circling my clit. I moan, so he continues just like that, letting out a sound of lustful appreciation. And with every noise I make, his enthusiasm grows.

Any time a man has eaten me out, I've always doubted whether they enjoyed it. I *know* Adam never did, since he always avoided doing it. But with Elliot—hell, with all three of these men—there's no doubt in my mind. It almost feels like they enjoy it as much as I do.

It's... freeing.

I rest my head on his thigh, and he grunts, his grip on my hips tightening. He's hard, his dick pressing against the zipper of his jeans.

That can't be comfortable.

Balancing myself with one hand, I use the other to undo the button of his pants. When I slide the zipper down, he stops.

"This is about you, Wren. Not me."

"Maybe I want this. As long as you want it, too."

With a squeeze to one of my thighs, he says, "There's no way I wouldn't."

It's difficult to push his clothes down enough to get his cock out, especially when he sucks my clit into his mouth, but I manage after a minute. Then I press a kiss to his hip bone before swirling my tongue around his tip. As I take him into my mouth, he groans, and it sends a rush of enthusiasm through me.

I move up and down gently, sucking lightly. My thoughts are hazy and slow, my focus split between the sparks of pleasure coursing through me and the way Elliot feels in my mouth.

After a few minutes, he thrusts into me, hitting the back of my throat. He swears, doing it again, his hands on my legs tightening.

"No," I say, grabbing onto his hips. "I want to take my time. Please?"

He gives me a long, slow lick. "You don't have to beg, love. I'm pretty sure I'd let you do anything you wanted to me." Then he goes back to sucking my clit, sending a shudder through me.

It doesn't take long before I'm close to coming again. With the way he's sucking and moving his tongue, there's no way I can last.

"Elliot," I gasp, popping his cock out of my mouth. I stroke him with my hand. "Oooh god," I say when he picks up his pace with his tongue.

My eyes slide closed, and it's all I can do to keep my hand moving as my orgasm hits. As I cry out, I bury my face in his thigh to muffle to sound. He lets up, pressing gentle kisses to my skin.

I go back to sucking his dick, taking as much of him in as I can without gagging. He doesn't try to take control, just lets out a series of groans. Then I feel him touching me, his fingers lightly brushing over my entrance.

"Shit, love. You're getting even wetter. Does this turn you on?"

"Mmhmm," I moan into his dick, cupping his balls. I'm enjoying this too much to stop.

"*Fuck.*"

It's the only warning I get, but the way he says it—strained and breathless—is enough of an indicator. I swallow his cum, making sure not to miss a drop, until his body goes limp under me.

Crawling off of him, I give him a grin and lick my lips.

"Don't do that again," he says, panting.

"Do what?"

"Muffle your cries when you come. I love the way you sound. And I want to hear you scream my name."

My cheeks heat. "But—but my neighbors will hear."

"Good." He sits up, pulling me closer and kissing me. "Then everyone will know who's giving you pleasure."

My mouth drops open, and he runs his thumb over my bottom lip. His eyes are still clouded over with want, and they drop to my body, taking in my breasts, my stomach, my legs.

"Fuck," he mutters. "One more."

He nips at my neck before running his lips down to my collarbones. Then he pushes me onto the bed so I'm on my back and he's hovering over me. I reach out to touch his arms, but he grabs my wrists and pins them to the mattress. With an appreciative sound, he leans down and licks one of my nipples.

As a whimper escapes my mouth, I arch my back.

"Did Adam ever make you scream, love?"

"Once or twice," I say on a breathy exhale, quickly followed by a moan when he sucks on my nipple.

"Are you going to scream for me?"

I giggle. "I think that depends on how good you make it."

"Oh, love. You just wait." He swirls his tongue in a torturously pleasurable way that has me squirming and moaning. When he switches to my other nipple, I'm pretty sure I'm so wet that I'm soaking the sheets beneath me.

Finally—*finally*—he rolls off of me, settling on his side next to me. He leans on his elbow, trailing his fingers down my body until I'm shuddering at his feather-light touch.

All on its own, one of my hands reaches down so I can find some relief, but he grabs it.

"Just because I let go of your wrists doesn't mean you can move them, Wren. They stay on the bed or I'll stop."

With a little gasp, I let my arm fall down, fisting the sheets instead.

He kisses the tip of my nose. "Good girl." And with that, one of his fingers brushes over my entrance, feeling how wet I am, before circling my clit.

"Say it again," I whisper. "Please. Please, Elliot."

He smirks. "I will. *After* you scream my name loud enough that everyone in the building hears."

Groaning, I shut my eyes, focusing on the way he's touching me. His mouth goes back to sucking on one of my nipples, and all of a sudden it feels like I could come really, *really* quickly.

I grip the blankets. "Oh god, Elliot, I'm so close."

He slows his finger, and I feel the beginnings of my orgasm slipping away. When I open my eyes, he gives me a devilish grin, slowly licking around my nipple.

"No," I whimper.

"You'll come when I say you can, love, and not a moment sooner."

Then he's back to circling my clit with his finger. Three more times, he brings me close to the edge, just to let it fade away again. By the fourth, I'm practically sobbing and begging him to let me come.

When he nods, finally giving me the permission I need, I fall so fast and so hard that it feels like I disconnect with reality for a moment. The scream is ripped from my throat, but I'm barely conscious of it.

When I come down, Elliot is watching me with a smile on his face. "Mesmerizing," he murmurs. "Absolutely mesmerizing. Such a good girl."

He kisses me, and my lips move against his sloppily. He doesn't seem to mind, though. In fact, he eats it up, wrapping me in his arms like he can't get enough of me.

When he pulls away, I gasp in a breath, clutching his arms.

"How are you feeling?"

"Better. Although I'm not sure if it's because of the orgasms or the pain meds."

"I don't care what the reason is, as long as you're in less pain." Sitting up, he pulls me with him. "Go pee. I'm going to get you some water."

In the bathroom, I glimpse myself in the mirror. After going about my business, I do my best to fix my messed-up hair and wipe the wild-eyed look off my face.

By the time I get back to the bedroom, I've caught my breath. Elliot is on the bed, still shirtless, propped up against the headboard.

"Come here," he says, patting the mattress beside him.

I do, slipping under the covers with him.

"Drink."

With a grateful smile, I take the mug from his hands and gulp down the water. Then he sets it on the nightstand and pulls me close.

PERFECT CONVERGENCE

I relax into him. How did I stumble across three men who make me feel so goddamned cared for? It feels too good to be true.

"Tell me about the three of you," I say quietly, running my fingers up and down his bare torso.

"What do you want to know?"

"Oliver told me a little about your relationship. You met in high school? Did you all fall for each other quickly?"

He laughs, a deep and soothing sound. "No. We were close since freshman year, though. I was the only one who knew my sexuality at that point. Rhett was vaguely aware that he wasn't just attracted to women, and Oliver . . . He fell first. And stayed in denial for the longest."

"Denial?"

"Mmhmm. Dated girl after girl for most of high school. But we all knew how he really felt. Even if he was trying to hide it from himself, too."

"Did you and Rhett get together first? Without Oliver?"

Elliot shakes his head. "No. Junior year, I finally admitted my feelings to them. Rhett and I talked about dating, but we both agreed to wait for Oliver. It just didn't feel right without him. He came around early senior year. After Sammy was killed, we all needed each other too much, and Oliver couldn't keep up the lie when we were all in so much pain."

Sammy. That must be Rhett's little sister.

"Was it hard? Seeing him in denial?"

For a moment, Elliot's silent. Then he sighs. "It was heartbreaking. He's always struggled with being confident in who he is, even though he's . . . god, Wren. He's fucking amazing. You don't even know the half of it.

"I think he was scared to mess things up since we were so close. But when he finally admitted he was as in love with us as we were with him, it was like this huge weight came off his shoulders. We were all still mourning Sammy, but at least he didn't have that holding him down too, you know?"

"Yeah," I whisper. "I never would've realized. Oliver acts so confident. And carefree."

"He's done a lot of work to accept himself." Elliot squeezes my arm. "And he's always been the fun one, so I guess you could call him carefree."

"I think you're all fun." With a smile, I look up at him. His expression is pensive, like he's lost in memories and only half here.

Then his gaze meets mine. "I bet you do," he murmurs before leaning down to kiss me.

There are still things I want to know about them, and Elliot seems happy to answer my questions, so I ask another one. "Oliver told me you've all been with other people. While you were with each other?"

He nods. "We used to have an open relationship. It was important to us, I think. We've always been committed to each other, but we all value our independence. We don't own each other. So seeing other people just . . . felt natural, I guess. Of course, we had boundaries. And we always made sure to prioritize each other, too."

"But you're not in an open relationship anymore?"

Elliot shakes his head. "What we do takes a lot of time and energy. And it's not always safe. Dating other people was fun, but we never found someone we were sure we could trust with every part of our lives. And it got to the point where we needed to focus on the three of us.

"Being with two partners is already a lot. It wasn't fair to the other people we were seeing, because we couldn't give them the attention they deserved. Especially when Oliver was dealing with some . . . mental health problems. And for me, personally, I never met someone who made me feel the way I do about Oliver and Rhett. So we closed things off. And that's how we've stayed since."

I wonder what mental health problems he's referencing, but I figure Elliot isn't who I should hear that from. Instead, I say, "Oliver told me you've never shared someone before."

Elliot smiles down at me. "He wasn't lying. None of us have ever been attracted to the same person the way we are with you."

I open my mouth, but then I close it. Do I desperately want to know *why* they're all attracted to me? Absolutely. But I don't want to fish for compliments when, in my opinion, I just got a pretty good one.

"You know how to make a girl feel special," I say, my cheeks heating.

He chuckles, kissing the top of my head.

With a sigh, I snuggle closer to him. He traces his fingers up and down my arm, and we fall into a comfortable silence. He's so warm and comfy. So . . . *safe*.

After a few minutes, my eyes begin to droop, and my head drops farther on his chest. "I'm sorry," I mumble. "I'm always so . . . tired . . . on the first day."

He strokes my hair, pushing it back from my face. Then he pulls the blankets over me. "It's okay, love. I'll still be here when you wake up."

I moan. And then, with his words reassuring me, I drift off within seconds.

I don't stay out for long. Thirty minutes, I think. Maybe a little longer. I moan, trying to roll over, but find myself still curled up in Elliot's arms.

"Hey." He kisses the top of my head. "I texted Rhett to come get me. We have some work to do tonight, and you need to rest."

"But . . ." I let the word hang in the air.

But what?

But I don't want you to leave.

But I don't want to sleep alone.

"It's for the best, love." As he says it, he smooths a hand down my back. "We have a lot of work to do tomorrow, but after that, we have a little break. Trust me, we'll make sure we see you before the week is over. Okay?"

"I'd like that," I whisper.

His phone vibrates, and he glances at the screen. "Rhett's here."

I make a move to get up, but he places a hand on my shoulder. "Stay in bed. I'll turn off the lights and make sure your front door is locked."

"Thank you."

He gets up, plants a lingering kiss on my head, and moves toward the door.

"Wait. Elliot?"

"Hmm?"

"I really like you. Like, really *really* like you."

With a soft smile, he says, "I really really like you too, Wren."

And then he's gone. I barely hear the sound of the front door closing behind him. The last thought I have before falling asleep again is that for the first time in a while, I finally feel . . . *happy.*

. . .

Unfortunately, that happy feeling doesn't last.

It would've been enough to get me through work if I didn't wake up to a text from my mom saying she's going to be in town for the next few days. *And* that she wants to meet for dinner tonight.

My shift goes by way too fast, and before I know it, I'm saying goodbye to Ava and trudging home. Going out with my mom is the last thing I want to do, especially since she'll probably harass me about Adam again, but how am I supposed to say no?

At least she said she's alone. I refuse to be in the same room as my stepdad. Not after . . .

I shiver. *Don't think about it, Wren. Don't do that to yourself.*

Once I'm home, I go through my post-work routine of showering, flopping onto my bed and scrolling through my phone in just a towel, and then scrounging around in the kitchen for a snack.

All it does is remind me that I need to get myself some dishes. And potentially a roommate. No. No, moving into a smaller apartment is the better bet, I think. Or maybe I could get a job in graphic design that pays better.

Could I? Could I actually do it?

I'd probably have to make myself a portfolio, but that's simple enough. I can work on it here and there in my free time. But would that do? I only have a minor in graphic design, since I majored in English. But at least I *have* a college degree, so companies won't turn me down because of a lack of one.

Before I know it, I'm scrolling through job ads for graphic designers in Philadelphia. I don't have a car, but there are enough public transportation options here that I'd be fine.

I bookmark a few promising jobs, and then I get ready for dinner, pulling on a dark pair of jeans and a pretty shirt. My mom chose a nice restaurant, which is odd considering she hates spending money, but whatever.

I put on more makeup than normal, knowing if I don't my mom will make some kind of comment about how I've let myself go. Then I give myself a once-over in the mirror, wishing I was going out with Ava or the guys.

The restaurant—some place called the Garden Grille—isn't too far away by subway, especially since I bring a book to read during the ride. Far too soon, I'm walking through the front doors, texting my mom to let her know that I'm here.

Turns out, though, I don't need to bother. The second I walk up to the hostess stand, I spot my mom, and my stomach drops to the floor.

She's not alone.

Adam's parents, Mary Anne and Robert, sit at the table with my mom, my stepdad, and . . .

Adam.

For a moment, I'm frozen to the ground, my heart in my throat. They're all chatting away, smiling at each other, except for Adam. His face is bruised, and one of his arms is in a sling. It takes me a second to remember that Rhett and Oliver are the ones who did that to him.

Without realizing, I take a step backward. *Get out of here. Get out of here before they see you. Whatever mom has planned, it's not—*

I bump into someone, almost losing my balance before I right myself. "Sorry—"

"Watch where you're going, young lady," a man snaps loudly. *Too loudly.*

It barely registers in my mind that the man I just ran into is Edgar Williams, a well-known businessman in the area. Because the next thing I know, my stepdad is out of his seat and walking toward me.

No. What the hell is he doing here? Mom said she was alone.

"Hello, Thomas," I say tightly as he approaches.

"Wren." He puts his hand on the small of my back, pushing me forward. I elbow him in the gut. He grunts.

"Don't you dare touch me, you piece of shit." Shoving his arm off me, I march to the table and glare at my mother. "What the hell is going on? I thought this was just supposed to be you and me."

"Well hi, honey. Nice to see you too." My mom stands and pulls me into a hug. "We're all just worried about you. We want to make sure you're not going to regret your . . . *life choices.*"

I pull away. "This is an intervention?"

"Well . . ."

Oh. my. god.

"No. No, I'm not doing this." With a shake of my head, I turn to go, but Thomas is blocking my path. "Seriously?"

"Sit down," he snaps. His arms are crossed over his chest, his face set with hard determination. If I was ten years younger, it'd have me quivering and obeying every single one of his commands.

Now? Fuck him.

I match his stance, leveling him with my own glare. "Typical. Going straight for intimidation tactics. I'm a fucking adult, Thomas. You have no authority over me."

"Sweetie," Robert says, turning in his chair to face me. "Please don't make a scene. We're genuinely concerned. I know it feels like an ambush, but it's not, I promise." Then he cuts Thomas a look. "Back off, Tom. You're not helping."

"Wren." My mom tugs on my arm. "Please?"

"Fine," I grit out. I plop into the seat next to Adam, scooching my chair closer to him since the empty chair on the other side belongs to Thomas. Adam sucks, but my stepdad is worse.

"Great," my mom says, giving the table a tight smile. "Wren, I ordered you a sugar-free lemonade. They have a great selection of salads here."

"Patricia," Robert murmurs, his eyes flaring wide in shock. As if her trying to make sure I watch my weight is new.

I flip open my menu. "Oh, wow, lots of pasta dishes, too. I think I'll go with one of those."

She gives me an exasperated look, but I don't care. If she's going to pull this on me, you'd better bet I'm going to give her shit for it.

When our server comes, we all order, and Robert and Thomas start up some small talk. Mary Anne tells my mom all about the garden she's planning on planting this summer, and Adam and I sit in uncomfortable silence.

I refuse to look at him, ignoring everyone once the food comes and diving into my cheesy plate of pasta.

It's not until we've all finished that everyone starts glancing at me nervously. Robert takes a sip of his drink before tugging at his tie.

I sigh. "Let's just get this over with. Lay it on me."

My mom gives me a horrified look. "That's no way to treat this! You need to drop the attitude. We're trying to help you."

I wave a hand around carelessly, slumping against the back of my chair. "So help."

Thomas clears his throat. "Wren, we all think you're confused. You and Adam were so happy together the last time we saw you. Talking about getting married and having kids, and you'd stay home and raise them—"

"As a woman should," my mom mutters.

"—while Adam takes care of and provides for the family. He's almost done with graduate school, and with Robert's connections, he's well on his way to a promising career."

"Maybe *I* want a promising career."

"Is there something wrong with staying home to raise children?" my mom snaps. "Honestly, Wren. I'm offended."

"I never said there was. But maybe that's not what I want."

Do I even want kids? I'm not sure.

"Who's putting these ideas in your head? Darling, you said you were excited to have children."

I pause. My hands close into fists under the table. Once upon a time, I thought I *was* on board with marrying Adam and raising our kids. But before him, what I wanted was so different.

As I look at the concerned group around the table, I'm forced to face the realization I had yesterday. The one I've been avoiding. The one that terrifies me and has me so stupidly disappointed in myself at the same time.

Instead of staying true to myself and sticking with the future I dreamed up for myself, I abandoned it the second I got into a serious relationship. Even worse, I shaped myself into the woman Adam wanted and somehow fooled myself into thinking I was happy with that.

I wasted three years of my life. *Three years.*

And I completely abandoned myself in the process.

"Maybe you're the ones who put ideas in my head," I say under my breath.

"What?" my mom says.

"Nothing. Look, I'm still young, Mom. I have plenty of time to figure out my life."

"You're twenty-four! Who knows how long it'll take you to find another man? Adam is here, and he loves you."

"She's already found three," Adam murmurs, low enough that only I hear him.

For the first time since I sat down, I turn and look at him. The man who cheated on me. Who threw a mug at my head. Who made me feel undesirable. *This* is what I'm supposed to want?

My thoughts must be written all over my face, because Adam looks nervous as hell. With his free hand, he reaches out and touches my arm. I flinch.

"Wren, I know we weren't perfect. I know *I'm* not perfect. But I love you, and I know you love me. We can work through our issues."

"I don't want to," I say flatly.

His hand falls to the table. "But—"

"No! Absolutely not. You know what you did, Adam. You don't deserve me." I roll my eyes at my mom's and Mary Anne's gasps. "I'm not confused, okay? I'm finally getting back to who I am. You just don't like it because I'm not trying to be who you all want me to be. But guess what, Adam? I'm not your type. And you are *definitely* not mine."

"Wren!" Mary Anne exclaims.

But I pay her little attention. Tossing my napkin on the table, I stand and grab my bag. "I'm done. None of you are here because you're worried about me. You're just trying to control me. Let me be who I am."

Then I'm heading toward the door, making sure to avoid Williams, who's also on his way out.

My mom calls after me.

I don't even look back.

Once I'm outside, I round the building. If I cut through the alley next to the restaurant, I can get to my subway stop faster. All I care about right now is getting out of here.

The alleyway is icy, but I managed it just fine on the way here. I go slowly, not wanting to slip and fall.

Maybe I'm too focused on watching my steps. Or maybe my mind is reeling from that ridiculous *intervention*.

Whatever the reason, I don't hear the footsteps behind me until it's too late, and a hand reaches out and grabs my arm.

Chapter Seven

Oliver

"What the hell is Wren doing here? Oooh. She doesn't look happy." I peer through my binoculars, following Wren as she takes a few steps back—directly into our mark.

We're in the building across from the Garden Grille, keeping a close eye on Williams. Once he makes a move to leave, Rhett and Elliot will leave and get a head start to cut him off on his road, which thankfully is pretty secluded. I'll follow Williams from a distance so we know if he makes any pit stops before heading home for the night.

It's supposed to be a smooth operation. Quick work. But I don't think any of us expected Wren to show up at the Grille tonight.

I watch as a man advances toward Wren. He puts a hand on her back, and Wren slams her elbow into his gut.

I smile. *Good girl.*

Eventually, Wren stalks toward a table. There are a few people at it I don't recognize, but one of them I definitely do.

"She's . . . meeting Adam."

"What?" Rhett snaps, and then he peers into the restaurant with his own binoculars. "Fuck. Who are the two couples? Parents?"

"Probably. Fuck, she doesn't look happy at all."

As I say it, Wren tries to leave, but the man who got up to meet her—her dad, maybe?—blocks her path.

"Son of a bitch," Rhett grits out. He's moving before the words are even out of his mouth, but Ell and I grab him.

"We can't show our faces here," Elliot reminds him. "We don't intervene unless she actually needs us. This may be our only chance to get Williams, and I don't want to fuck it up."

Rhett's grip on his binoculars tightens so much I think they might snap in two. But he stays put, his shoulders bunched up.

I let out a worried sigh. Williams is at his table, so I split my time between keeping an eye on him and watching Wren. Everyone at her table seems tense, and she looks like she might explode—or burst into tears.

"I don't like how close she is to him," Rhett murmurs after a few minutes.

"What's worrying me is how much she's leaning away from the other guy," Elliot says. "Don't like that one bit."

We keep an eye on her while both tables order and get their food. At some point, Adam places his hand on Wren's arm, and she flinches.

"I'm going to kill him. Fuck forcing him out of town. I'm going to gut the guy."

Elliot and I exchange a glance but keep our mouths shut. At this point, if Rhett wants to take out Adam, I'm not sure either of us would stop him.

Wren shoots out of her seat, and I'd be lying if I said the shocked looks on everyone's faces aren't funny. Then she storms out of the building, not even bothering to look back.

Which, I suppose, is why she doesn't notice Adam getting up and following her.

Rhett swears. Then Elliot is tucking his binoculars away.

"Williams is leaving. Rhett, we have to get to the car. Oliver, make sure you don't lose sight of him."

"Got it."

We exit the building, hoods up, sticking to the shadows. But we all freeze when we hear a feminine voice shout, "Adam, let me GO."

"Fuck," Elliot mutters. From where we are, we can't see Wren, but there's no doubting it. That was her voice.

"I'll get her," I say. "I have a minute before Williams gets to his car, and then I'll catch up." I'm already on the move.

"Cover your face," Rhett says gruffly. God, he's pissed.

I don't have to look at Elliot to know he hates this. Any deviation from the plan is a potential catastrophe. But this job can *technically* be done without me—as long as nothing goes wrong.

I cross the street, slipping on my ski mask, eyes darting over the empty sidewalk.

Where are you, princess?

"You." *Thud.* "Are." *Thud.* "SO." *Thud.* "STUPID." *Thud.*

I don't realize I'm running toward her voice until I skid to a stop at the mouth of an alleyway. A few yards in, Adam is on the ground, scrambling to get up but slipping on the ice. Wren is standing over him, gripping a book in her hands and bringing it down on his head.

Adam grunts. He must give up on getting to his feet, because instead, he hooks an arm around her legs and yanks.

She falls on her ass. As she cries out, her book flies into the air and lands a few feet away.

I'm on Adam in an instant, pulling him away from Wren and throwing him to the ground. With a kick to his nuts, I leave him groaning, turning to Wren. She's already up on her feet, snatching at her book and backing away.

"You stay the hell away from me," she snaps.

Seriously? I just saved her.

Right. Ski mask. She probably thinks I'm going to mug her.

"This is why I don't do the planning," I grouse.

She narrows her eyes, tilting her head the way she does when she's curious or on the verge of figuring something out.

Did she recognize my voice? Fuck. She literally ran into Williams inside. If she knows I was here tonight, and then Edgar dies before the night is over, she'll put the pieces together like it's nothing. Or at least she'll suspect. There's no way his death won't be all over the news.

"I don't have any money," Adam moans. "But she's probably got a tablet in her bag. Always has it on her for her books and shit."

She glares at him. "You're a piece of shit, Adam."

I kick him in the ribs, and he yells in pain. Then I reach for Wren.

Yelping, she smacks my hand away with her book. "Don't touch me."

I wrench it from her hands and grab her wrist. "I'm trying to help you," I grit out, lowering my voice so she doesn't recognize it.

"Wren? Adam?" a masculine voice calls.

Her eyes widen. "No. Not Thomas," she whispers, taking an involuntary step back.

"Here," Adam yells, slowly crawling to his feet.

Shit. I'm running out of time to get to my car. And there's no way I'm leaving Wren. Not when she looks as terrified as she does right now.

I'm going to have to take her with me.

To her credit, she tries to run. Even stomps on my foot before she does. But she doesn't even make it a step before I'm grabbing her and pulling her into me. My arms wrap around her torso, trapping her arms to her sides.

"Stop," she shouts, wiggling and trying to stomp on my foot again. "I swear, if you kidnap me, and another stupid fucking *man* gets in the way of me finally living my goddamned life, I'll—I'll... do SOMETHING!"

My whole body shakes from silent laughter. Is that seriously where her mind is going right now? God, she's cute.

"We need to work on your self-preservation instincts," I murmur.

She freezes. "Ol-"

I clap a hand over her mouth before she says my name. Adam can still hear us. "It's me, princess," I whisper in her ear. "And I need you to run."

I let go of her, grab her hand, and pull her down the alley. There's a shout behind us, I presume from whoever the fuck Thomas is, but I don't look back.

At the end of the alley, I turn left onto the sidewalk, then wrench open the passenger door of my car and shove Wren inside. By the time I've shut myself into the driver's seat, the man Wren elbowed inside the Grille comes bounding out of the alley, followed by a limping Adam.

I've never been more grateful for darkened windows in my life.

Wren shrinks down in her seat as I yank off my ski mask.

"Who is he?"

"My stepdad," she pants as he looks our way. "Oh god, oh *no*—"

"He can't see us. Just take deep breaths. I've got you. I promise." As I reach out and take her hand, I peer at the parking garage exit. In under a minute, Williams' driver is pulling his car out and onto the street.

Thomas and Adam are still looking up and down the road full of parked cars, searching for Wren. Starting my car will draw their attention, but if they don't get out of here soon, I won't have a choice. Williams is probably already waiting at the restaurant door. Picking him up won't take long.

Get out of here, guys. Get out of here now.

I've already fucked up by revealing my identity to Wren. Everything else has to go smoothly tonight. But what else was I supposed to do? Hurt Adam? What if it got pinned on Wren? And I certainly wasn't going to leave her there.

"Wait." She turns to me. "What were you doing here? And why were you wearing a mask? You scared the living hell out of me!"

I give one last glance to Adam and Thomas. Thomas has his phone to his ear, and he's speaking rapidly. *Shit.* Did he call the cops? At least it looks like they're heading back to the restaurant.

"Turn your phone off. To them, it looks like you got kidnapped, and we can't have anyone trying to track you."

She huffs, obviously annoyed, but at least she listens.

Once Adam and Thomas are out of sight, I turn on the car and pull out, heading the direction that Williams' car went.

"Were you following me?" There's a hint of fear in her voice.

"No! More like a ... wrong place, wrong time situation." After a pause, I say, "Or maybe right place, right time."

"I'd say I was managing fine on my own, but I guess I wasn't."

"Never thought I'd see a book used as a weapon." I smirk at her.

She laughs. "Oh, and my self-preservation instincts are fine, by the way. I *was* trying to get away from you."

"Yeah, because you didn't want another *stupid fucking man* ruining your life. I think staying alive should be a higher priority, princess."

She huffs. "I suppose." Then, turning to look at me, she says, "Thank you. I ... I probably could've told Adam off. Or outrun him, considering he's still all beat up. But Thomas ..."

When she trails off into silence, I grip the steering wheel. I have no idea what went down in the restaurant, or why she dislikes her stepdad, but none of it's good. And I hate how scared Wren looked earlier.

"He was going to propose," she murmurs after a minute or so. She's staring out the window, running her fingers over her seatbelt. "He was cheating on me, but he was still going to *propose*. I don't get it."

"That's ... fucked up."

We lapse into silence, and I'm able to catch up with Williams' car and keep a safe distance.

After a few minutes, Wren says, "Um. Oliver?"

"Yeah?"

"Where are we going?"

Right. I still have to give Wren some kind of explanation. God, Elliot is going to be so pissed.

Shit. I need to call him.

"Hold on, princess. I'll answer you in a second. But I just remembered I need to call Ell."

Thankfully, my phone is hooked up to the car, so it's easy to dial. He answers on the first ring.

"Hey. Where are you? And is Wren okay?"

"Just pulled onto the interstate behind Williams. Looks like he's headed home."

"And Wren?"

I don't miss the unease in his voice. Fuck, I should've called them immediately. They've probably been worrying this whole time, wondering if she's safe.

Which she's *not*. Not when she's with us tonight. Especially since, by dragging her along, I'm making her an accessory to fucking murder.

"There's . . . been a slight change in plans."

"What?"

I clear my throat. "Say hi, Wren."

"Hey Elliot," she says cheerfully, but she casts me a concerned glance.

There's silence on the other end of the line. I can picture Elliot sitting in the passenger seat as Rhett drives, trying to think his way out of this.

If Tyler wasn't in the picture, it'd be a simple decision: I follow Williams until he turns onto his road, and then I take Wren home. But Tyler is a wild card, and Rhett and Elliot may need backup.

But if they *do* need backup, there's a chance we're endangering Wren. And if things go wrong...

After a minute, Elliot sighs. "It's too big of a risk."

"We'll be fine," I protest. "The plan is damn near perfect. Williams and his men will be sitting ducks."

"I'm not risking getting her killed," Elliot says.

"What?" Wren looks at me with a shocked expression, and then she narrows her eyes, and my god, she reminds me so much of Elliot when she's thinking hard. Then her jaw drops. "Oh my god. Are you guys going to kill him?"

Elliot swears. "We can't involve her in this. O, you need to follow Williams to the checkpoint and then head home."

"*I* am a part of this conversation," Wren says, glaring at the speakers. "If you need Oliver for your plan, there's no way we're turning back."

I try to hold in a laugh. The fact that she stands up to him with such ease makes me proud. He can be an ass when he gets stubborn.

"Wren—"

She ignores him. "Oliver. Do they need you?"

"It'll be safer for them if I'm there."

"And what are the odds of you and me ending up in danger?"

"Wren," Elliot snaps. "Stop. This isn't up for negoti-"

"What are the odds?" she asks me.

"Low. Ell, from my position, we'll be able to see anyone coming for us from way off. *And* I can keep you two safe from a distance if anything goes wrong. That was always the plan."

"I can't risk her safety."

"Well, I'm not willing to risk yours," Wren says.

A mixture of relief and pride swells in my chest. She's adapting so quickly. And not freaking out at all, which is honestly fairly surprising.

Elliot sighs. "There isn't anything I can do to stop you. Just... be careful. And if it comes between running and fighting, Oliver, you get her the hell out of there."

"I know. I'll call you back when he's closer."

Elliot hangs up, and I let out a long breath, staring ahead at Williams' car. I'm far enough behind that I'm probably not even registering as a threat to his security team.

"So you're hitmen?"

I nod. "I can explain later. But right now, I need to get you up to date on our plan, okay?"

"Got it."

I give her the details, explaining every tiny step.

The spot we picked to ambush Williams is, for all intents and purposes, perfect. At the intersection where they'll turn onto his road, the far side is woods, and the side we'll drive past is a field surrounded by more trees. Conveniently, there's a hunter's stand on the edge that gives me a perfect view of the spot where Williams' driver will be forced to stop.

Earlier today, we explored the woods and found a decently sized tree limb that fell down during a storm. We dragged it to the edge of the forest that's right by the road, and Rhett and Elliot will haul it onto the road after hiding their vehicle.

From there, it's simple: kill everyone as quickly as possible and then get the hell out of there.

I'll be in the hunter's stand, where my hunting rifle is already waiting for me, so I can pick people off from a distance if I need to.

The idea, though, is that I won't have to.

As we drive down the interstate, Wren asks me question after question. She sounds a little nervous, but for the most part, she's rolling with the punches and putting on a brave face.

There are a few things I'm worried about, though.

"We'll have to run through the dark. Will you be okay?"

She's quiet for a second. Then, "You'll be with me the whole time, right?"

"Yes. You're not leaving my sight."

At my words, she relaxes into her seat a bit. "Then I'll be okay. It's not as scary when I'm with someone else."

With a nod, I let my head fall back onto the headrest. This job should go smoothly, but I still don't like having Wren with us. Especially since . . .

"Wren. We're going to be killing people. It . . . have you ever seen a person die before?"

"My grandma," she says. "But she was in a nursing home. This is different. I—well, I was kinda figuring I just wouldn't look. You want me watching your back, right?"

"I think that's for the best." The last thing I want to do is traumatize her tonight. If we haven't already.

I'd imagine realizing your three partners are all killers isn't an easy pill to swallow. Yet she's acting pretty damn calm.

The rest of the drive, we stay quiet, except for a couple times when she asks me a question to clarify something. I keep one hand on the steering wheel and the other on her leg, my thumb rubbing her thigh.

When we're finally nearing Williams' road, I call Elliot again. He and Rhett are in position in the woods. I've already slowed my speed, so by the time Williams' car takes the last curve before the intersection, I switch off my lights, peering into the darkness, thankful for the little bit of light coming from the moon.

By the time we're pulling up to the field, Williams' car is just turning onto the road. I throw the car into park and grab the keys, and then Wren and I are out and running toward the hunter's stand.

She stays quiet and low, just like I told her to, until we reach the ladder. I go first, grabbing my rifle and getting into position. Through the night vision scope, I watch as one of Williams' bodyguards gets out of their stopped car and circles to the front, glaring at the tree limb in their way.

Any second now.

I could pick him off with ease, but our hope is that Tyler will get out of the vehicle to help move the limb. It's not the end of the world if he doesn't, but it sure would be convenient.

Williams' first bodyguard says something, turning to the car, then rolls his eyes. He's a big guy, so I'm not surprised when he's able to grab the limb and pull it toward the edge of the road. He struggles, but he's managing.

So much for Tyler getting out.

Two shots ring out—one for the bodyguard, the other hitting one of the car's tires. The driver still tries to back up, so I shoot out one of the back tires, too.

More shots, these ones from the car, but Tyler is shooting blind. He has no idea where Rhett and Elliot are.

One of the back doors opens as Tyler keeps shooting. Just as Elliot predicted, they're going to try to get to the woods for better cover.

I watch as Tyler bolts from the car, jumping the ditch and sprinting into the trees, shooting wildly as he does.

What the hell?

Did Tyler just . . . abandon his uncle?

I watch, waiting for Rhett and Elliot to emerge from the woods and finish the job, but nothing happens. Tyler is gone, probably running for his dear life, so what are they waiting for?

Unless Tyler actually managed to hit them.

No. *No.* That can't be right. Tyler is smart, and we all know that. Ell and Rhett are probably just waiting to make sure he's actually running. Stepping out of the woods would be a stupid thing to do right now.

I take a few deep breaths to calm my rapidly-beating heart. This is *not* the time to freak out.

I shouldn't've stopped taking my meds.

After a minute, the driver's side door opens, and Williams' driver creeps out. He's gripping a gun in his hands, but it's pretty obvious by the way he's holding it that he's not familiar with firearms. And why would he need to be? He's just the driver, technically not part of Williams' security detail.

No one shoots him.

Elliot and Rhett are safe. They're just not shooting him because he's not a threat. That's all.

There's no way Tyler shot them. They're smart enough that they would've taken cover the second he started shooting blind. And now that he's in the woods, there's no way they'd let him sneak up on them. They'll be watching their backs.

"Oliver?" Wren whispers.

I keep my sights locked in on the driver. "Yes?"

"I—I think I saw something in the field. Coming toward us. But I'm not sure if I'm just imagining things." Her voice is shaking.

The reality of the situation must be setting in. For all I know, she's never even heard a gunshot before.

I'd give her some type of comfort if I could, but I have to stay focused. "Just keep looking. Let me know if you see anything closer."

"Okay," she whispers.

The driver creeps around the car and opens the back door that's facing my way. Williams slips out, staying low.

And that's when it clicks. Rhett and Elliot must be trying to lull them into a false sense of security. Get them to think that it's safe to get out of the car. Then I can shoot Williams from a distance.

See? They're fine. Just thinking. Elliot is good at that.

"Um, Oliver—"

I take out Williams with a single shot. The driver yells as his boss drops to the ground, pointing his gun into the darkness, before I take him out, too.

There's a yelp behind me, and then a loud thud. *Shit.*

Whirling around, gun ready, I find Wren hovering in the doorway of the stand.

"I didn't see him until he was on the ladder. It was too dark. I—I'm sorry, Oliver." She backs up, her eyes on the snowy ground below.

I peer down, using my scope to see in the dark. Tyler is scrambling to his feet, holding one hand to his face. "What did you do?"

"Kicked him in the face," she whispers. "He fell down."

"Good girl," I murmur. "Now look away."

She does, and I shoot Tyler in the chest. He flies back, landing in the snow.

For a moment, I stare at him. When I shot out that tire, he must've realized it came from behind the car. He's smart—there's no way he hasn't noticed the hunter's stand before.

So if he came here, maybe he didn't even realize Rhett and Elliot were in the woods.

Or he already killed them, and he was coming after us to finish the job.

The thought leaves a hollow feeling in my chest. We knew Tyler could pull something like this. They knew what to expect. But still, *what if—*

"Oliver." Wren puts a hand on my arm, shaking me lightly. "Didn't you say we needed to get out of here fast?"

Fuck. She's right.

No one lives near this stretch of road, all of the houses spaced out with miles in between them. But there's still a chance that someone could drive past and spot us.

"Yeah. Yeah, we've gotta go."

I put the rifle in its case and go down first. Tyler's body is still, his eyes wide open in shock. Wren descends the ladder, and I help her over his body, but not before she gets a glimpse of him.

For a second, she freezes, clutching my arms. Then she shakes her head and grabs my hand, and we take off toward the car.

Normally, we have to clean up and dispose of the bodies. But the man who hired us for this job wanted us to leave a mess behind. "I want it plastered all over the news," were his exact words.

None of the guns can be traced back to us in case we somehow lose one in a fight. Hell, neither can these cars—they're not the ones we normally use, and they're not registered in our names.

I start the car, checking my phone, but I can't bring myself to move.

They were supposed to check in by now. Elliot should've called.

Maybe they're still hiding. They don't know I shot Tyler.

"Oliver? Are you okay?"

I look at her, but my mind barely registers her form, or the worried expression on her face.

"Oliver, we have to go."

"I can't lose them," I say. It's a struggle to get the words out of my mouth. My chest is tight, and it feels like my lungs are filled with lead.

Wren gives me a terrified look. And then she's getting out of the car, coming around, and opening my door. "C'mon," she says, pulling me out. "I'll drive. Give me your phone."

She walks me around to the passenger side, getting me situated before climbing into the driver's seat. Then she's turning the car around and driving back the way we came while hitting a few buttons on my phone.

After a second, she places it between her ear and shoulder, tapping her fingers on the steering wheel. I try to focus on her face, on the way her hair is wrapped up on top of her head. But it does nothing to stop the panic growing in my chest.

"Rhett didn't answer," she murmurs, tapping the phone screen and holding it to her ear again. She takes the curve in the road gracefully, biting her lip. "Elliot isn't answering either."

Shit. Fuck. No.

"Oliver, I need you to tell me what to do. Do we go back and try to find them? Is there any reason why they wouldn't answer?"

"We keep our phones on silent while we work." I get the words out in between short breaths.

It's possible they didn't see her calling.

"Okay. But everyone's dead, right? The job is over?"

I nod as a tear makes its way down my face. "They don't know that."

Or they're dead.

Fuck. They're dead.

"Okay. Okay, so do we go back?"

"No." I rub my face with my hands, soaking them with my tears. "No, we can't risk getting caught. Someone may have heard the gunfire."

Wren is silent for a moment. Then she places a hand on my thigh. "I'm sure they're okay."

She sounds about as confident as I feel.

And it pulls me deeper into my panic.

Chapter Eight

Wren

Each breath Oliver gasps in is like a stab to the heart. His hands are trembling, and when I grab one of them, it's drenched with tears.

The road is dark and winding, so I go slow, not wanting to slide on a patch of ice and end up in a ditch.

To be honest, I have no idea how I'm staying so calm. But I have one thought and one thought only right now: get as far away from that mess of a crime scene as possible.

As we approach a stop sign, I peer down the road. "Oliver, do I go straight here? Or turn? I don't remember."

He doesn't answer, and when I've come to a complete stop, I turn to him. "Oliver," I whisper, squeezing his hand, but I don't think he even hears me.

"I can't lose them. I can't. I can't live without them."

His phone vibrates in my lap, and I snatch it up. "Rhett?"

"Where are you?" he demands.

"I . . . I don't know."

"Are you *safe*, Wren."

"Oh. Yes. I'm safe. Oliver. Hey, Oliver. Rhett is okay." I give him a small shake, and he looks at me, but he doesn't *see* me.

"She's safe, Ell," Rhett says. Then, "Is Oliver okay?"

"No. No, not at all."

Rhett swears.

"Shit. Sorry. He's fine physically. But I think he's having a panic attack. Rhett, I don't know where we are. And he's not in a state to tell me where to go." I glance in the rearview mirror. It looks like we're alone, but it feels like we're being watched.

You're just being paranoid, Wren.

"Describe where you are to me. Are there any landmarks? Road signs?"

"I'm at a stop sign." Then I look up. "At . . . Jefferson and Pineland. Woods to my right, a field to my left."

"That's good, Wren. You're in the right place. Turn left. I'll guide you to our meeting spot, okay?"

"Okay." I look around, not turning yet. Still alone. So why does it feel like we're not?

"You're going to take that road for a few minutes. Is Oliver able to talk?"

"Um. Hang on." I set the phone down in my lap and turn to Oliver. "Hey. Rhett and Elliot are okay. They're safe, Oliver."

He looks at me. Blinks.

"Do you want to talk to Rhett?"

Gulping in a breath, he nods. So I hand him the phone, watching him for a second. His eyes slide closed when Rhett starts talking, and he slumps into his seat.

Then I get going, turning left after checking our surroundings one last time. Oliver says a couple words, but it sounds like he's struggling to get them out.

After a few minutes, I tap his leg. "I need to know where to go next."

His eyes widen. "I don't—I don't know where we are. Oh god, I—" He stops speaking, and I hear Rhett saying something through the phone. Oliver inhales through his nose, then exhales, and then repeats.

When he hands the phone back to me, I let my fingers brush over his. He's still shaking, but it's more like shivering now. I don't know if that's better or worse.

"Wren?"

"Hey. I just passed a farm, I think? There was a silo."

"Okay. You're doing really well, sweetheart. Up ahead, there's another stop sign. You're going to go straight there, okay?"

"Got it. Um. Rhett?"

"Yes?"

"I'm really scared."

I've been trying to ignore it, but that feeling of being watched keeps creeping back. It's as if, at any second, the darkness around us is going to swallow us whole.

If Oliver was doing okay, I'd probably be able to keep it at bay. But it's like my fear is feeding off of his, and if I don't find a distraction, I may end up in a puddle of panicked tears, too.

"What do you need, sweetheart?"

"Tell me where we're headed. Are we going home?"

"No. We have to hide the cars first. There's a cabin about forty minutes out. Well, less than that now. We're meeting there."

"Is it yours? The cabin?"

"Ah, no. But a friend is letting us use it. And the cars. We help each other out when we need it."

"Is he . . . like you guys?"

"Yeah. Sort of."

I slow at the next intersection. "Straight at the stop sign?"

"That's right, sweetheart. You can do this."

We go on like that for the next half hour, him distracting me and giving me directions. Oliver's breathing evens out, and he stops shivering, but he stays quiet.

Eventually, I notice another vehicle approaching from behind us. Panic spikes in my chest.

It's a road. People drive on roads.

The thought doesn't calm me at all.

"Rhett? There's someone behind me." I know it's stupid, and I hate that I sound like a scared little kid, but Tyler's face flashes in my mind, his eyes open and his chest blasted open and bloody.

What if there was someone else who saw the whole thing?

"It's us, sweetheart. You're safe. I promise."

"It's you?"

"Yep. And we're at the cabin. See the orange mailbox on the right?"

"Yeah."

"Turn into the driveway after it."

It's narrow, but at least it's plowed. The driveway is surrounded by trees on each side, and I have to drive for a minute before the cabin comes into view, deep in the woods.

I slow to a stop and throw the car into park. Undoing my seatbelt, I turn to Oliver and take his face in my hands. "We made it. We're all safe. Everyone's okay, Oliver."

The only response I get is a deep breath, which honestly is a relief to hear. For a while, his breaths were so short and shallow, I thought he might pass out.

I hear car doors slamming shut, and then the crunch of snow and ice. Oliver's door opens, and then Elliot is leaning in, unbuckling his seatbelt and pulling him out of the vehicle.

My heart aches at the way Oliver clings to Elliot, and at the sob that rips through the night air. Rhett comes up behind Oliver, wrapping his arms around both him and Elliot, so Oliver is sandwiched between them.

"We're okay," Elliot says, smoothing his hand down Oliver's arm. "We're all safe."

"I thought you were dead." Oliver's voice breaks.

Tears fill my eyes. The way these three care about each other is like nothing I've ever seen before.

I can't lose them. I can't.

Chills run through me when I realize that, if I hadn't been in the stand with Oliver, *he* may have been the one we all lost tonight. The only reason Tyler wasn't able to sneak up on Oliver is because I was watching and managed to kick him down the ladder.

The image of Tyler laying in the snow, shirt soaked red and with blood trickling out of his mouth, sticks in my mind. I try to push it away, but I can't. The way his eyes were still open, the way blood was all over his face from his broken nose—I can't distract myself from it.

Maybe that's why the nausea feels so sudden.

One second I'm in the car, watching Elliot and Rhett comfort Oliver. The next, I'm on my hands and knees on the cold ground, heaving up everything in my stomach.

"Shit," I hear someone say, and a few seconds later a hand is pushing back my hair. "You're okay, Wren. I know it's a lot. I know."

Elliot helps me stand, and I glimpse Rhett still holding Oliver from behind. His arms are wrapped around his chest, and he's murmuring something quietly into Oliver's ear.

There's no one from my childhood or teen years who I'm that close to anymore. I can't imagine knowing someone from such a young age and then almost losing them. And it must be so much worse, considering they've all been in a relationship for so long.

"Oliver," I whisper, stepping toward him. But Elliot takes my hand.

"Let's get inside. It's too cold to keep standing out here."

We head into the cabin, and Elliot switches on the lights. He directs me to the bathroom, where I find some mouthwash to get the taste of puke off my tongue.

When I come back into the main room, Oliver is on the couch, slowly sipping from a glass of water, and Rhett is starting a fire.

"Where's Elliot?"

"Moving the cars into the garage," Rhett says as he strikes a match.

I frown. It's dark outside, but there's no way I missed an entire garage out there.

At my confused look, Rhett says, "It's underground."

"More like a bunker, really," Oliver says. "Finn likes to be prepared."

He holds out an arm to me, pulling me close when I settle next to him. I take a deep breath, inhaling his woodsy, vanilla smell.

"I'm sorry I freaked out on you, princess. It was pretty terrible timing."

"Are you okay?"

Oliver sniffles, then gives me a tired smile. "I'll be fine. We're all safe. That's what matters."

Standing, Rhett watches as the kindling in the fireplace catches. "I hate that Tyler got away. We couldn't see him once he ran into the woods. I don't think he even bothered looking for us. Just got the hell away as soon as he could."

"Actually . . ." I exchange a glance with Oliver just as the front door of the cabin opens and Elliot steps through.

"Tyler came after us," Oliver says. "My guess is he realized someone was shooting from behind them when I shot out one of their back tires. Is that why you guys took so long to check in? You weren't sure where he was?"

Rhett nods. "What happened?"

"I kicked him in the face," I say.

Oliver gives me a proud kiss on the cheek.

"He got that close?" Elliot comes around to stand next to Rhett. He looks as panicked as Oliver did when they weren't answering their phones.

"It was my fault," I blurt before either of them try to pin this on Oliver. "Oliver was busy doing... well, shooting. Whatever happened over there. It was so dark, I didn't see Tyler until he was on the ladder of the hunter's stand."

"And Wren is the only reason he didn't fucking kill me," Oliver says. His voice is stronger now. "So the lecture you have coming our way? Save it."

Elliot's jaw snaps shut. Then, "He's dead?"

We nod.

For another second, Elliot stays tense. Then he blows out a breath and runs a hand through his hair, and his face softens. "I'm just glad you two are okay. I was worried."

He steps around the coffee table and pulls me up. When his arms encircle me, I lose myself in his soothing citrus and sandalwood smell. I didn't realize how tense I was until I relax into him.

Tears prick my eyes, but I blink them back. Rhett and Elliot already had to deal with Oliver breaking down. I don't want to give them one more emotional burden.

"You were really brave tonight, Wren," Elliot says, pressing his lips to my forehead. "I'm proud of you."

Fuck. The tears come back, and this time it's harder to calm myself down. I need some sort of distraction.

"What happens next?" I ask, looking between the three of them. Oliver looks absolutely exhausted, but Elliot and Rhett look as alert as ever.

"After a finished job, normally we celebrate," Elliot says. "But Wren, I'm sure you have a lot of questions, and—"

Tyler's body flashes in my mind again, and my empty stomach turns. "Celebrating sounds great. How do you normally do that?"

Oliver grins lazily. "With sex."

"Oh."

"Unfortunately, I'm much too tired to do anything but watch. But it's lucky for us, those two—" he nods to Elliot and Rhett, "—like to be watched. What about you, princess?"

My body is still a little shaky from throwing up, and emotionally, I'm in shambles. "I don't think I'm up for it, either."

"That's okay, love." Elliot gives me a reassuring kiss. Then he does the same to Oliver, and it's so tender it melts my heart.

Oliver rubs his hands together. "Oh, princess. You have no idea what you're about to witness."

Chapter Nine

Wren

We all move to a bedroom, and Oliver settles into an armchair in the corner, pulling me onto his lap. It faces the bed, almost like its sole purpose is for what we're using it for right now.

Elliot and Rhett circle each other, watching each other like predators sizing up their prey. Over the weekend, they both showed their rough side, but I've never thought what would happen when you put two dominant people in a relationship together.

Leaning into Oliver, I whisper, "They're not going to kill each other, are they?"

"I wish we had popcorn," Oliver mutters in my ear. "It's always entertaining to watch these two go at it and see who gives in first."

"Who gives in first?"

He nods. "You'll see."

"You're not going to make this easy, are you?" Rhett says, giving Elliot a dark, lustful look.

"When do I ever?"

With that, Elliot grabs Rhett and shoves him onto the bed, straddling him. But in a split second, Rhett has them flipped over so he's on top, pinning Elliot's wrists to the mattress. Elliot tries to dismount him, but it's in vain.

"All bark, no bite, huh, pretty boy?" Rhett says. Then he releases one of Elliot's wrists and grabs his jaw. "Open up."

Elliot smirks. With one of his hands free, he's able to struggle for control again. He grabs Rhett's arm—the one holding his wrist—and yanks. As Rhett falls, Elliot somehow flops him onto his back.

He throws me a glance over his shoulder. "Someone's a little too cocky, huh, Wren?"

My jaw drops, and Oliver snickers. *Holy shit.*

Rhett and Elliot continue to struggle for the upper hand, managing to get in hot, branding kisses while yanking each other's clothes off.

"This is intense," I whisper to Oliver.

"Oh, this is nothing, princess. I'll have to make sure you watch sometime when Rhett brings out his knife."

My eyes must bug out of my head, because he has to hold back a laugh.

When I look back to the bed, Rhett has Elliot on his back with his head hanging off the edge of the mattress. Rhett stands above him, holding his wrists in the air, while Elliot catches his breath. He's grinning.

"You tried, pretty boy. You tried. Would you like a gold star? Maybe an extra pat on the back?"

"Fuck you," Elliot pants out.

"Elliot likes this, right?" I whisper.

"Being forced to submit and being degraded? Depends on the person he's with. That person being Rhett."

"Open up that sassy mouth of yours. You're going to take every drop of my cum down your throat tonight."

Elliot grunts, but he obliges, opening wide. Rhett slides into his mouth with a groan before pulling out and then thrusting into him again.

"Oh my god," I murmur.

Oliver squeezes my arm. "Hot, right?"

Nodding, I rub my thighs together. I've never watched like this before, but if the butterflies in my stomach are any indication, I like it.

Rhett fists Elliot's dick, and they both moan. He falls into a rhythm, pulling out occasionally so Elliot can recover while he continues stroking Elliot's cock. After a few minutes, Rhett pulls out again and crouches, murmuring something in Elliot's ear. I don't hear his reply.

Standing, Rhett looks to me. "Would you like to make him come, Wren?" He smiles when I nod. "Get on the bed."

I obey, my eyes not leaving his hand, watching the way he's working Elliot's dick. He still has Elliot's wrists restrained with his other hand.

"Do exactly as I say. Understood?"

I nod. He's so . . . in control. And it's very, *very* attractive.

"Sit in between his legs. Perfect. Elliot, spread your legs more. Wren, how wet are you?"

Blood rushes to my cheeks. "Very."

"Get your index and middle finger wet. Absolutely soak them."

My eyes widen. Is he—*oh god.*

"Have you changed your mind?"

I shake my head.

"Then don't keep him waiting, sweetheart."

With Rhett and Oliver watching me, I undo my pants and slide my hand into my underwear. After I've coated my fingers, I pull them out, holding them up and showing Rhett. They glisten in the light.

"Start with one finger. Gently."

With my index finger, I circle his hole once, twice, getting it lubed up. Then I slide it in slowly. Elliot moans, his fists clenching, and I look to Rhett.

He nods, so I keep going, moving my finger in and out until Elliot loosens up a bit.

"Add the second."

I do, gently, little by little.

"Relax, Elliot."

He does, taking a few deep breaths. My fingers move in and out of him with ease.

"Find his prostate and massage it with your fingers. Rub them against it."

When I find it, Elliot grunts. I rub it lightly, not sure if too much will hurt him since I've never done this before.

Rhett is still stroking his dick, watching his face with a smirk. "You like her fingering your ass? Gonna make you come?"

"Fuck," Elliot grits out. "More."

"Add a little more pressure, sweetheart."

I do, and Elliot lets out a loud moan. It sends a wave of pride through me, knowing I'm partially responsible for it.

Once I find a rhythm, it doesn't take long before Elliot comes all over his stomach and Rhett's hand. When Rhett nods to me, I pull out my fingers.

"So messy," Rhett chides, staring at the cum on his fingers. "You'd better clean it up, pretty boy." He holds his hand out in front of Elliot's face, and I watch with fascination as Elliot licks it clean. "Now get on your knees. You have a job to finish."

Elliot moves to the floor quickly, kneeling in front of Rhett and taking his cock into his mouth with a moan. Swearing, Rhett lets his head fall back, and his eyes slide shut.

"Just like that, Ell. Maybe I'll give you two gold stars."

With a strangled grunt, Elliot continues, grabbing onto Rhett's thighs for balance. I glance to Oliver, and he seems enraptured by the sight of Elliot on his knees for Rhett.

"You ready?" Rhett says after a minute, his voice strained. "You're too fucking good at this, Elliot."

"Mmhmmgh."

With a groan, Rhett comes down Elliot's throat, just like he said he would. When he pulls out, he falls to his knees, taking Elliot's face in his hands and kissing him roughly.

"Next time," Elliot pants, "I'm in charge."

Rhett smirks. "We'll see."

Chapter Ten

Rhett

Elliot flops onto the bed, still breathing hard. I sit in between him and Wren, leaning down to give him another kiss. This one is slower. Less rough. More meaningful.

Some of the bullets Tyler shot into the woods were terrifyingly close to us—more so than we'll ever tell Oliver. Our job comes with risks, and we all know that, but normally we're able to stay relatively safe.

We knew Tyler was an extra danger, and we decided it was a risk worth taking. But after the ordeal we put Oliver through, and my own fear of losing Ell in the moment, I'm not so sure.

We're going to need to be extra careful, especially since we have Wren now.

"I love you," Elliot murmurs against my lips.

"Mmm. I know." I give him one last kiss before turning to Wren. She's watching us raptly, her lips slightly parted. "Did you enjoy that, sweetheart?"

She nods, her eyes meeting mine slowly.

"Do you want more?"

That seems to bring her back to reality. She blinks. "Oh, I'd rather not. As long as—as long as that's okay. I don't think I'll be able to get out of my head."

I kiss her temple. "It's always okay to say no to us, sweetheart."

"Always," Elliot murmurs, and Oliver nods in agreement.

The way she relaxes at our reassurance unnerves me. *As long as that's okay.* Who made her think she couldn't say no? That she had to ask fucking *permission* to not have sex?

I make a mental note to figure out whoever it is, find them, and gut them. Then, with a gentle kiss to Wren's forehead, I turn back to Elliot. "Shower?"

He nods.

There's a bathroom attached to all the bedrooms here—Finn made sure of it when he built this place. After Wren uses it to wash her hands, I pull Elliot into the shower.

I grab the soap, rubbing it all over his body, cleaning every inch of him. When he steps under the water, I do the same for myself.

The first time I tried to take care of Elliot after sex, he was confused, saying he didn't need my help. Now he enjoys it, and I happen to know that me cleaning him up afterward is one of his favorite parts.

"One of us needs to stay with Oliver tonight," he says eventually, quiet enough his voice doesn't carry back into the bedroom. "It can't be Wren. I'm not convinced he won't break down again."

I nod. If I thought I'd be much help, I'd volunteer. There are certain things I can do when Oliver has a panic attack—hold him, help him to breathe, stuff like that. But I also tend to freeze up in the moment. Elliot is much better at . . . *emotions.*

A lot of the time, I just make things worse.

"I've got it." He squeezes my arm. "But Wren might not be in a much better state. She stayed calm for as long as she needed to, and we gave her a good distraction, but that's all coming to an end real damn fast."

I swallow hard. "I can handle it."

Elliot doesn't acknowledge the lack of confidence in my voice. Instead, he nods and shuts off the water, and we dry off and get dressed.

In the bedroom, Oliver is already under the blankets, sound asleep. Wren sits next to him, stroking his hair. I don't miss the slight shake in her hand.

"Hey, love. I'm gonna stay with Oliver tonight."

Wren jumps, as if she was so lost in thought that she didn't notice us walk in. "Oh. Hi. Yeah, okay." With one last kiss on Oliver's forehead, she climbs off the bed. "Will he be all right? He was so scared." She blinks rapidly, and then she sniffles.

"He will. C'mere, love."

She practically melts into Elliot, still trying to hold back tears. I'm not sure what all went down earlier, but it'd be a lot for anyone. She went from going to dinner with her family to almost getting killed in the span of a few hours.

"I'll be okay," she says, and her voice is stronger and more determined than I expected.

When Elliot lets her go with a chaste kiss, she smiles up at him. Then she turns to me, a questioning hesitancy reflecting in her eyes.

That's when I realize I've tensed up.

Aside from the phone call earlier and me telling her what to do to Elliot, we haven't talked since I dropped off those pain meds for her yesterday morning.

One second, I was fine, and the next, everything felt like it was moving too fast. The way Wren looked at me after I handed her the pills was too caring, too *intimate*. My skin felt like it was on fire, and it took everything in me not to bolt out of there.

Now, I look between Elliot and Wren, working my jaw. This is *not* the time to freeze up. Underneath his collected exterior, Elliot is exhausted. I can't dump Wren's reaction to tonight on him. He needs to rest.

"Come with me," I say as gently as I can. Then I turn and walk out of the room and down the hallway.

The kitchen is dark, so I flip a light on. My guess is Wren is hungry, considering she puked up most of her dinner.

Was I worried about her all night? Yes. Ever since I laid eyes on her in the restaurant and saw that deer in the headlights look on her face, I've been nothing but *consumed* with worry.

But how do I tell her that? How do I tell her that she means much more to me than she should? And how do I say that she's handling this shitshow like a champ?

"Are you hungry?"

She grimaces, wrapping her arms around her waist. "No. But I should probably eat."

"How about something light?"

She nods, watching me cautiously.

Just tell her how you feel. Say something. Anything.

But I don't. I turn, rummaging through the cabinets, until I find some canned soup. When I hold it up, she nods.

I dump the soup into a pan and light the stove.

The silence between us is so uncomfortable, it's making my skin crawl. Which is exactly what I was trying to *avoid*.

Hearing her yell at Adam earlier sent a spike of fear through me. I was so afraid he was hurting her, or worse. And it caused me literal pain to not immediately rush to her side.

I trust Oliver—of course I trust Oliver. But it didn't stop me from worrying. And now, knowing how close Tyler got to her... Things could've gone so differently tonight. For all of us.

Fuck. I have to do something.

I spin around to look at her, and she's standing exactly how she was a minute ago, frozen, still hugging herself. She looks so small, so scared, so overwhelmed.

What would've happened if we hadn't been there to intervene when Adam came after her? What would've happened if she hadn't been in the hunter's stand with Oliver? Or if she hadn't been watching the ladder?

Stop. Stop with the what ifs. She's safe. Everyone is safe.

I step toward her.

Fuck this.

"Rhett—"

Before she can get another word out, I take her face in my hands, tilting her head upward, and press a kiss to her forehead. "You have no idea how fucking worried I was about you."

She throws her arms around me and buries her head in my chest. Like this, with her completely enveloped in me, she feels so small. I suppose, in comparison to me, she is.

She doesn't say anything. Just breathes me in, her body quivering as she tries to collect herself.

"Tell me what you need, Wren. Tell me what you need and I'll give it to you. Anything."

"I don't know." She clutches my shirt in her hands and looks up at me with watery eyes. "So much happened. I—you—I've never seen someone die like that before. There was blood everywhere. And it was so dark, and Oliver was so upset, and I didn't know where to go. I was so scared, Rhett."

I tighten my embrace. "I know. I know you were scared. But you kept it together. You got here, and you're safe now."

She sobs. "I'm sorry. I'm trying not to cry, but—"

"Hey." I smooth her hair back from her face. "It's okay to fall apart now."

"I don't want to—to make you uncomfortable."

"Let me worry about that, sweetheart. Tonight was a normal night for me. But for you? Hell, Wren, you've been through something a lot of people never have to experience in their lifetime. It's okay if you're struggling."

She squeezes her eyes shut, and tears fall onto her cheeks. Tenderly, I brush them away before turning off the stove and pouring the steaming soup into a bowl. Then I lift her and set her on the counter so she's closer to my eye level.

"It felt like someone was watching me," she whispers. "Like we were going to get lost in the darkness and never find our way out again."

"And now?" I wipe under her eyes, where her mascara has smudged. "How do you feel now, sweetheart?"

She pauses for a second, and I search her eyes as she blinks up at me. "I feel . . . safe. Right now. But what about the future? Is it always this scary? Am I going to constantly be worrying about you guys? What if one of you gets hurt? Or dies?"

"We're always careful. This was a little more of a risk, but—"

"But what if something *does* happen, Rhett? What if I get mixed up in another job, but this time things don't work out?"

"We'll do whatever is necessary to keep you safe. That's what we do for each other, and that's what we'll do for you."

She shakes her head, and I watch as she struggles with the panic that's fighting to take over. "What if—what if you can't find me? Or what if you're too late? What if I get lost again, but this time I can't find my way back? What if I forget who I am again?"

I'm not sure what she means, but it doesn't sound like she's talking about what happened tonight anymore. She's catastrophizing, and I don't know how to stop her.

There's only one thing I can think to say.

"Wren." I lean my forehead against hers. "I don't think you understand that if, somehow, we lost you, we'd burn the whole world to the fucking ground to find you again."

"Because that's what you'd do for each other?"

"Yes. And you're a part of us now. We take care of what's ours."

She slumps against me, and I pull my arms tighter around her. It's a lot for anyone to take in, and honestly, she's doing well.

For a while, we stay like this. There are no sobs or cries, but I can feel her tears silently soaking my shirt. My hand moves up and down her back in what I hope is a soothing motion, praying desperately that this is what she needs.

Eventually, she murmurs, "I think I'll be okay."

"Your soup is probably cool enough to eat."

As she slips off the counter, I find her a spoon.

"Are you tired, sweetheart?"

She nods. Then she leans over the bowl of soup, blowing on it. "Are you?"

"Yeah. But I won't be able to sleep."

With a frown, she stares at her soup. "Do you know why you have insomnia?"

The muscles in my back tense up. "It's a long story."

She glances at the butterfly tattoo on the back of my hand. For a second, it looks like she's going to ask me a question, but then she turns back to her food.

I know Elliot told her about Sammy. She has questions, I'm sure. And we'll tell her eventually—we have to, considering half of our time is spent getting revenge on the man who killed her. But it's too intensive of a topic for tonight.

Once Wren is done with her soup, I take her hand. "There's another bedroom at the end of the—"

"No."

"What?"

Her hand tightens around mine. "Can I stay with you? I know you're not sleeping. But I don't want to be alone. Please?"

Right. Of course she doesn't want to be alone. Why didn't I think of that? "Sure. Let me get you a pillow and some blankets."

As I head toward one of the bedrooms, I peek in on Elliot and Oliver. O is still sound asleep, with Elliot holding him from behind. Safe. Peaceful.

When I come back into the living area, Wren is sitting on the couch with her chin propped on her knees, her arms wrapped around her legs. She's so far gone to the world that she jumps when I drape a blanket around her shoulders.

"You can sleep here. I'll stay with you until you fall asleep. If I leave the room, I won't go far. I promise."

She hugs the pillow I hand to her. "Thank you, Rhett."

Kneeling next to the couch, I take her hands in mine, pressing my lips to her fingertips. I'd hold her while she falls asleep, but I don't want to disturb her when I inevitably get up at some point. And I don't know how much more touching I can handle tonight. "I'm proud of how well you handled everything today, sweetheart."

"Rhett," she whispers.

"Hmm?"

"Kiss me."

Tangling my fingers in her hair, I capture her mouth with mine. She grabs my arms to hold me close to her, matching the desperation that bleeds into every one of my movements.

I know I'm not everything you need. But I'll never stop working to be. I don't want to lose you.

When I break off the kiss, she gasps in a breath.

"Wren," I murmur, barely opening my eyes to take in the sleepy, content look on her face. And then my mouth is on hers again, and I'm wondering if, with this kiss, I can communicate all the words I can't seem to force out of my mouth.

Her little sighs warm my heart, soothing the ache in my chest that appears whenever I think of Sammy. This time, she moves away first, her fingers tracing lines over my face. When she yawns, I push her down onto the couch.

"How are your cramps? Do you need pain meds? Or water?"

After I realized on Monday how little I know about periods, I spent the better part of the day reading every article on them that I could get my hands on. Drinking enough water seems to be pretty important.

"I should probably have some water, yeah."

I grab her a glass, and after she takes a couple sips, I set it on the coffee table. "Sleep, Wren. I'll be here if you wake up."

With a moan, she pulls the blankets over her body, wiggling deep into the cushions. "You promise?"

"There's nowhere I'd rather be."

Chapter Eleven

Elliot

When I wake, Oliver is still sleeping, clutching me to him like I might disappear at any moment. I brush my fingers down his arm. He doesn't stir.

His panic attack last night was concerning to say the least. Not only was the timing potentially dangerous, but it's also the first one he's had in a long time. Which has me wondering if he stopped taking his meds again.

I have a feeling I know just what triggered him to do it.

"Ol." I give him a little shake.

He groans, his hold on me loosening. Then his fingers dig into my skin and his eyes fly wide open. When he sees me, alive and unharmed and next to him, he relaxes, whispering, "Thank fuck."

I give him a chaste kiss before sitting up. "We should get moving. There's supposed to be a snowstorm around two, and I want to make sure we miss it."

With a yawn, he rolls over, looking at the clock on the nightstand. It's a little after eight. "I should probably shower."

We get up, brushing our teeth before Oliver turns on the shower, and I step into the hallway. The smell of coffee drifts from the kitchen, and my stomach growls. With everything that happened last night, I forgot to eat dinner. Hell, we all did.

In the living area, I find a full pot of coffee ready and waiting. After pouring myself a mug, I look around. The place is empty. So where are—

"Oh god. Oh *god*."

I laugh into my mug before taking a sip of the coffee. *That's* where they are.

Back down the hallway, I stop in front of an open door. Inside, I see Wren bent over the bed with Rhett kneeling in between her legs. He has his fingers moving in and out of her, and there's a trail of blood dripping down her leg.

There's a towel discarded on the floor. It looks like Wren just got out of the shower.

"Let me guess," I say, sipping my coffee and stepping into the room. "He saw blood and turned completely feral."

Wren moans as Rhett tosses me a smirk over his shoulder. His face is smeared with red.

There's a short dresser on the far side of the wall. I walk over and lean against it, taking in the view.

Wren is completely bare, groaning into the mattress. Rhett seems to be taking his time, spearing her with his fingers and rubbing her clit with his other hand.

"Please, Rhett. Please."

"I'm not done yet," he says, pulling his fingers away and giving her a long, slow lick instead.

"How long have you had her on the edge for?" I ask.

"Not long enough."

Wren screams frustratedly into the bed, fisting the sheets.

"Do you want my cock, my beautiful whore?"

"Yes," she cries.

"Mmm. My guess is you want Ell's too?"

When she turns her head to look at me, her eyes are wild. Desperate. "Yes, please."

"I dunno, Rhett. Doesn't sound like she wants it that bad."

My comment earns me a death glare, and I have to stop myself from laughing at her misery.

"Do you want his cock buried down your throat? Like what I did to him last night?"

"Yes," she sobs.

Pulling away, he says, "In a minute."

He stands, pulling her up with him and getting red on her arms. Then he turns her around, smearing blood over her breasts.

I'd stop him, but I know he wouldn't do this without her permission. He knows very well that not everyone is into blood play.

"Perfect," Rhett mutters, half to himself, looking Wren up and down. "Fucking perfect."

Setting my mug on the dresser, I step toward them. "You want us to take you at the same time, love?"

She nods.

"Do you think she's earned it, Rhett?"

He looks down at her, watching as her eyes widen with the fear of him saying no. But there's also a hint of delight.

"I think she still needs to work for it. On your knees, sweetheart."

I grab the towel and place it at her feet, not wanting to get blood on the floor. She drops onto it, placing her hands on Rhett's thighs and staring up at him.

"Is this where you belong, sweetheart? On your knees for us?"

She nods, reaching up to undo his pants. When she has his cock out and in her hand, she glances up at him questioningly.

"Go on."

Slowly, she licks the underside of his dick from base to tip before swirling her tongue around his crown. The whole time, she maintains eye contact with him, and he groans. As she takes him into her mouth, he runs the pad of his thumb over her cheek, leaving behind some of the blood that's still on her fingers.

"Fuck."

He must be having one hell of a time.

As Wren sets a pace with her mouth, my dick presses painfully against my pants, so I undo them. It's not long before I'm stroking myself while watching Wren take Rhett's cock beautifully.

When he juts his hips forward, she gags. I soak it all in, not wanting to ever forget the way they look right now.

"You suck my cock so well, sweetheart. Should we give Ell a turn?"

She moans in protest, gripping his thighs tighter, picking up her pace. *Fuck,* she's enjoying this that much?

"Hmm. So you don't want us to take you at the same time?"

She lets out a pleading sound, pulling back and releasing him with one last suck that has him hissing in a breath. "I want it. Please."

"Then you'd better do as we say, hmm?"

"Yes," she whispers.

Rhett moves out of the way, and I step up to her, pulling her hair out of her face.

"You ready for more, love?"

"Please." Then she opens her mouth for me, and I slide into her mouth with a groan.

She sucks my tip gently, swirling her tongue, before moving up and down. I don't know when exactly she figured out that I prefer my dick to be handled much more gently than Rhett, but I'm just happy she did.

She moans when I hit the back of her throat. It's hard to stay still, but I'll be able to fuck her mouth soon enough. For now, I let myself enjoy the feeling.

Rhett gets on his knees, reaching in between Wren's legs. Her whimpers vibrate through my dick, and my grip on her hair tightens.

Pulling away from her body, Rhett stares at his blood-coated fingers, mesmerized. And then he's spreading it over his chest and stomach, his eyes glued to the way it stains his skin.

Wren gasps in a breath when I hold her head and pull out. She leans forward, trying to keep going, but I shake my head. It felt too good, and I'm not ready for this to be over yet.

Hooking my arms under hers, I pull her to her feet. Her gaze snags on Rhett's chest, murmuring a quiet, "Oh my god," under her breath.

She has no idea how big of a deal this is for him—that she's willing to let him cover himself in her blood, that she's willing to wear it on her skin, too.

"Get on the bed, Wren. The way Elliot was last night."

Her eyes light up as she does what he says. Rhett crawls onto the bed with her, placing a pillow under her hips and spreading her legs.

Wren props herself up on her elbows. "The sheets."

"Don't worry about it. They're dark for a reason." He slides two fingers into her, satisfaction blooming in his eyes when her breath hitches. "Lay back, Wren. That's it. Such a good girl."

Her head is hanging off the edge of the mattress, ready for me. Suddenly, I wish I had ropes to tie her up with. I know Finn has some around here somewhere, but I much prefer mine. They're softer, whereas Finn has a sadistic streak and has rougher ones.

Wren whimpers when I trace a finger down her throat. Then she opens her mouth without me even having to tell her to, sticking her tongue out.

Just then, Rhett pulls his fingers out of her and lines up his cock with her entrance. He rolls his hips forward slowly, and I watch Wren's face. She said her period isn't bad after the first two days, but I still want to make sure she's comfortable.

"Jesus fuck," Rhett groans once he's slid in all the way. He presses tiny circles to her clit with his thumb. Then he moves in and out slowly, letting Wren adjust. "Tell me if this is okay, sweetheart. I don't want to hurt you."

"It's good," she says breathily. "It's—ohhh. Please don't stop. Please, Rhett. I want to come this time."

He grins, grabbing onto her hips.

I brush my cock against her lips. "What do you do if you need a break, love?"

"Tap your thigh," she whispers.

"That's right."

She opens her mouth again, and I slip inside. Her hands grip the sheets at the bottom of the mattress by her head.

Rhett and I both start off slowly, gently. But soon Wren is whimpering, and her back is arching off the bed. Rhett's gaze is fixed on where he's moving in and out of her, blood probably everywhere.

When Wren sounds close, I pull out, wiping some drool from her lips. She's breathing hard, and her whole body is riddled with tension.

"Rhett, I'm so close. Oh god, *ohmygod*."

For a few more seconds, Rhett continues pounding into her. Just when she's about to break, he slows, his thumb leaving her clit.

"No," she cries.

That's when I notice the shadow in the doorway.

Oliver steps into the room, taking in the scene. "Having all the fun without me, huh?"

"Oliver," she pants. "Please, I want—I want to come so badly. They won't let me come."

Rhett lets out a dark, low chuckle. "I don't know why you're begging him, sweetheart."

Oliver's eyes run over her blood-covered skin. "You agreed to this?"

She nods.

He shrugs. "Sorry, princess. Looks like you got yourself into this mess. You're going to have to get yourself out of it." Then he turns to Rhett. "You look like a kid in a candy store."

Rhett grins. "That's exactly how I feel."

Wren yelps when he pinches her clit. Then he goes back to circling it with his thumb, and she practically melts into the bed.

"Do you think she's earned it, Ell?"

"I think she has." Crouching down, I hold Wren's head and kiss her. She moans as Rhett starts thrusting into her. "Do you want me in your mouth again?"

She nods. "Harder, please."

I raise an eyebrow. Sometimes, it feels like she likes things just as rough as Rhett does. "You want me to make you choke on my cock?"

"Please."

Oliver groans. He's leaning with his back to the wall, his hands shoved in his pockets. It's a nonchalant position, but there's a lustful fire burning in his eyes.

When Wren opens up for me, I thrust into her, hitting the back of her throat. She gags, and I let up for a second before repeating the action until tears are streaming down her face.

Her fingers brush my thigh, and I pull out.

"You good?"

She nods, and then she cries out. "Rhett, oh god. I'm going to come, please let me. Please, oh *fuck*." Her eyes roll into the back of her head.

I press her shoulders into the mattress, holding her down as she explodes. She bites one of her hands to stifle her cries, but I yank it from her mouth. We all want to hear how she falls apart.

As she reaches her peak, she screams Rhett's name, and I watch as he slows, fighting not to come. *Fuck.* If I was inside her right now, I don't know if I'd be able to hold myself together.

Finally, Rhett removes his thumb from her clit, and she sags into the mattress. He's still rolling his hips into her slowly, watching the way her chest heaves up and down.

The way Wren comes is always explosive. But this? This was way more intense. And . . . addictive.

After a few more seconds, Rhett grabs her and pulls her up so she's straddling him, positioning her until she's sinking onto his cock. He reaches in between them, and she jumps when he touches her clit. But then he pulls his hand out, his fingers covered in blood again, before wrapping it around her throat.

With a happy sigh, she grabs onto his shoulders and begins riding him, eyes shut. He keeps a firm grip on her throat, his butterfly tattoo partially covered in blood.

"Look at me, Wren. Look at me when you're fucking me."

She opens her eyes, and her expression softens when she meets his piercing stare. Then she kisses him, which I think is a surprise to us all considering his mouth is covered with blood.

He groans, his fingers digging into her hips. Then he throws his head back, swearing as he comes inside her. Wren's expression lights up with fascination and ecstasy as she watches Rhett's face. And then he falls back, pulling her with him, panting.

"Fuck, Wren. Fuck."

She brushes her nose against his with a soft smile. The simple action has my heart warming in my chest.

Crawling off of Rhett, Wren glances to me. There's blood all over her thighs now, but she doesn't seem to mind. In fact, if anything, she looks more enthusiastic.

"Ready for more?"

She nods.

Rhett pulls himself up so he's sitting to one side of the bed, leaning against the headboard. I push Wren onto her back, spreading her legs and gently brushing my finger over her clit. Once we get going, I know I won't last long, and I want her to come again. So I work her until she's writhing underneath me.

When I slide into her, we both moan. It's messy, but I don't really care. I want to be inside her, and I know Rhett will enjoy seeing me all bloody, too.

I keep my movements even, not going too slow, but not going terribly fast, either. With every thrust, Wren's breasts bounce, and she lets out a soft whimper. I don't let up on her clit, watching as she struggles to last longer. But I can't hold on for long.

Oliver crawls onto the bed, naked. His fingers trace around her nipples, not quite touching, just teasing. Wren's breath hitches, her back arching into his touch. Then he brushes the pads of his thumbs over her nipples, watching with delight as she shudders.

When he pinches them lightly, it pushes her over the edge. I feel her clenching around me, and it only takes a few more pumps before she pulls me under with her.

My orgasm washes over me so powerfully that I almost fall forward. It's not just her, although that's a huge fucking part of it. No, it's *us*. Rhett's eyes on me, Oliver watching both of us, and Wren squirming underneath me. All of us on the bed, together like this. It's an unlikely convergence of four people from clashing backgrounds, and yet we fit. Almost perfectly.

I think she sees it in my eyes, because she reaches out, placing her hand over mine where I'm fisting the sheets. Something soft and warm and so goddamn caring shines in her eyes as I come down from my high.

"Shit," I mutter.

She sits up, cupping my face in her hands. There are so many emotions swelling in my chest as she kisses my cheek tenderly.

"C'mere, Ell." Rhett pats the mattress next to him.

Whenever Rhett is open to affection, I fucking take it. So after squeezing Wren to me for a few seconds, I settle next to Rhett, as close to him as possible. As he puts an arm around my shoulders, his cedar and sage scent envelops me, and I breathe it in.

"Hi, princess." Oliver gives her a smile.

"Oliver." She rises to her knees, throwing her arms around him.

With one hand holding the back of her head, he presses his lips to her forehead, scrunching his eyes closed. I could see it written all over him yesterday, how disappointed he was in himself. How bad he felt for freaking out on Wren.

She pulled through, though.

"Wren, it's okay if you can't handle more. If—"

She presses a finger to his lips. "There's absolutely no way I wouldn't want you, Oliver."

He relaxes into her. She pushes him onto his back, taking his already-hard cock in her hands and stroking.

"Sometime soon," Rhett whispers in my ear, "you and I should tie them up at the same time. Tease the shit out of them and see who breaks first."

"I heard that," Oliver says, shooting Rhett a glare. But then he grins. "I'm down."

Wren giggles. Then she crawls on top of Oliver, lining his cock up before lowering herself onto him slowly. Once she's settled on top of him, she sighs happily, looking down at him. "You know, you're really cute."

Turning his head to look at me and Rhett, he says, "You hear that? She thinks I'm cute."

Wren snorts. "Don't let it go to your head."

"Too late," all three of us say at the same time.

She throws her head back in a full laugh, and I think it's safe to say we're all completely enraptured by it. Then Oliver thrusts upward, and she falls forward with a surprised yelp. But he grabs her hands, holding her up and not letting go.

"Let me," she whispers, gazing down at him.

He nods, and she begins grinding her clit against him, moaning as she does. The way they look at each other is so intense, so genuine, so caring, that for a second I think Wren might start crying.

But she closes her eyes, taking a deep breath. Then she smiles down at him, keeping her pace slow, like she wants to savor every single second.

When she comes, it's quieter than the other times, more like she's drowning than exploding. Oliver follows soon after, still holding her hands, refusing to break eye contact.

For a moment, neither of them move. Something passes between them silently before Wren finally looks down at herself.

She laughs, taking in all the blood. "I don't know why I even bothered showering."

Chapter Twelve

Oliver

We all have to shower again, and after that, Rhett makes us a quick breakfast. Once we're ready to leave, we head into the basement and then into the garage. Again, it's really more like an underground bunker. Finn is involved in some wild, dangerous shit. This cabin is only one of his safe houses.

Wren looks around at everything, especially at how well-built the place is, but she doesn't say anything. Instead, she quietly follows and then climbs into the back of Elliot's SUV with me. We stashed it yesterday so the unregistered cars will stay here.

Once we're on the road, it seems to click for Wren that we're heading back to real life. And that today is, in fact, just another Wednesday.

Who could blame her?

She smacks her forehead. "Oh my god! I was supposed to work today. Oh, fuck."

Rhett turns to look at us from the passenger seat. "They won't fire you, will they?"

I hand him my phone, nodding to the article I pulled up. Ever since I saw Thomas barking into his phone, I've been suspicious that he called the authorities. This morning, I found evidence that he did.

Peering over Rhett's shoulder, Wren's mouth drops. "Local woman kidnapped under mysterious circumstances. They think I was kidnapped?!"

"Why wouldn't they?"

"I mean, I literally *ran away* with you."

"They probably thought you were scared and didn't know what else to do." I blow out a breath. "My god, I'm glad I had you turn off your phone. You haven't turned it on, right?"

She shakes her head. "Haven't even touched it."

"Good. We'll help you with a cover story." I pull her into the seat next to me, tucking her under my arm and buckling her in. "But for now . . ." I meet Elliot's gaze in the rearview mirror.

"We know you have a lot of questions for us, Wren," he says. "And we have some for you. We can try to hash some of this out on the drive home if you'd like."

"Questions for me?" She glances between the three of us. "Like what?"

"Like what the hell you were doing with Adam last night, for starters," Rhett grits out. His expression turns dark.

I cringe. His frustration isn't coming from a place of jealousy. It's just that he was worried about her—and that he absolutely hates Adam's guts. But his reaction is still harsh.

Wren doesn't seem hurt, though. She leans forward and squeezes his arm. "I didn't know he'd be there. My mom invited me to dinner with just her. But it was actually an intervention, I guess."

Ah. That explains why she looked so pissed at the Grille.

"For what?" Elliot asks. His eyes are on the road, but his grip on the steering wheel tightens.

"For . . ." Wren sighs. "It's a lot."

"We have time, princess."

"They—my mom, my stepdad, and Adam and his parents—didn't think I was making a good decision by breaking up with him. They kept saying that my future with him is what I wanted, and I was making a big mistake by leaving him.

"But the thing is, I . . . I *didn't* want that future with him. Not ever. I made myself believe that I did. But before I met Adam, I never wanted to be a housewife. I never wanted to be a stay at home mom. *He* is what I needed an intervention from. It just took me a couple years to realize it."

"What did he want when he came after you?" Rhett's voice isn't as hard, but it's still tense.

With a sigh, Wren leans into me. "He was still trying to convince me. My mom told me he was planning on proposing before I broke up with him."

"Elliot, you'd be proud," I say. "When I got to her, she was beating Adam over the head with a book."

He laughs, and the idea even puts a small smile on Rhett's lips.

I almost ask about Wren's stepdad, but then I remember how terrified she looked yesterday when she saw him.

Another time.

Instead, I give her a proud grin. "Now, for you. What questions do you have?"

Her expression turns pensive. With a hint of worry, she says, "Is it always as nerve-wracking as last night?"

"God no. We knew there was an extra risk with this job, but we took it because Edgar Williams is—*was*—a grade A scumbag." *And it furthers our plan.* "And we have Elliot. He's a fantastic planner. Can think his way out of anything. We always make sure we're safe, princess."

Wren nods slowly, absorbing everything I just told her. "So it's true? You guys kill people for—for money?"

Dread fills my stomach. This is what we were afraid of. That she'd find out, get freaked out, and then want nothing to do with us. We're professional killers, after all. It's scary to know someone can take a life over and over again.

"We do, princess. Does that bother you?"

For an agonizing moment, she's silent. Then, after her eyes have trailed from me to Elliot to Rhett, and then back again, she says, "What if the person doesn't deserve it? To die?"

"Simple. We don't take the job."

It's something we decided on years ago. Losing Sammy caused us so much unnecessary pain. What's the point in avenging her if we become as bad as the man who killed her? So we're picky about what jobs we take, and in the process, we take out some of the world's worst pieces of shit.

Wren seems to relax at my answer. "Do you travel a lot?"

"A few times a month."

"Have you ever gotten close to getting caught?"

I hesitate. By the police? No. But by other people? Once, years ago. But Elliot and Rhett don't like talking about it. Probably for the same reason I can't bear the thought of losing them.

"We're always thorough, love," Elliot says.

She nods. And then she settles into me further, one of her hands resting against my chest. "I think that's all the questions I have. For now."

Within twenty minutes, her breathing deepens. It's a long drive home, and my guess is she slept terribly last night, so I keep my arm wrapped around her to hold her steady. It's the least I can do after yesterday.

I can't believe I lost it on her. Couldn't even fucking drive. It felt like my heart was going to explode in my chest. Like I was going to die if I never saw Ell and Rhett again. And there was Wren, right after going through a bunch of traumatic shit, and she kept it together. She stayed calm when I couldn't.

Am I proud of her? Immensely. But I can't lie, I hate myself for falling apart at such a terrible time. Not only did she need me to stay in control, but I was a mess. A complete fucking mess.

Elliot and Rhett never would've started panicking like that.

Ever since we all realized we were attracted to Wren, I've had my doubts that it would work. Not for me, anyway. Rhett and Ell have their problems, but they're manageable. But me? Sometimes I feel like I'm more of a burden than anything else.

I'm strong, sure. But not in the way Elliot and Rhett are. I'm smaller. Softer. Not nearly as dominant. Probably closer to a sheep than a wolf. And I'm not always... *stable.*

Elliot catches my gaze in the mirror. Knowing him, he's already figured out exactly what's going on in my head, so I look away. I don't want to talk about it.

I know I'll have to eventually—he'll force it out of me. And if he doesn't, Rhett will. But for now, they let it go.

At some point during the drive, it starts snowing, but I barely notice. I settle against my seat, still holding Wren, and let the comforting sounds of Elliot and Rhett having a quiet, low conversation wash over me.

Eventually, I fall asleep, the chant of *they're safe, they're safe, they're safe,* the last thing I remember.

Chapter Thirteen

Wren

"It's time."

I glance up from my book. It's Friday evening, and after a nice dinner at the guys' house, we all settled into the living room for a quiet night.

Well, all of us except Rhett. He's been especially contemplative all day, and now he seems restless.

Elliot nods, his gaze fixed on Rhett. "You think so?"

"She needs to know. I'd say she's proved herself, wouldn't you?"

All of them look at me. Rhett from where he's standing, Oliver from where he's draped sideways in an armchair, and Elliot from his spot on the love seat next to me.

"Uhhh . . ." I squirm under their stares. "What?"

My phone buzzes in my pocket. After pulling it out and seeing it's my mom calling me *again*, I silence it. I texted her to let her know I'm safe, but I have no desire to talk to her after what she pulled on Tuesday night.

One of my neighbors texted me to let me know that my mom showed up at my apartment the other day. Thankfully, I wasn't there—the guys haven't wanted me to wake up alone from my nightmares, so I've been staying with them.

It's been a hectic couple of days. Elliot concocted a cover story for me, so when I "turned up," I told the authorities that my kidnapper just let me go, and that I never saw his face. The police chalked it up to my kidnapper grabbing the wrong girl, just like Elliot predicted they would.

Sitting straighter, I say, "What do I need to know?"

There's more?

"You have the dress, O?" Elliot asks.

"Of course I do."

Elliot stands, offering me his hand and pulling me up. With one hand against my lower back and the other tilting my chin up, he kisses me so softly, so sweetly, that my knees almost go weak. "Go with Oliver. We have something to show you."

I give him a questioning look, but he ignores it as Oliver shuffles me into the hall. We head upstairs, and once we're in his bedroom, he disappears into his closet.

"Oliver, what's going on? What do I need to know?"

"You'll find out, princess. In the meantime," he says, stepping out of the closet with a red dress and black heels in his hands, "let's get you all dolled up."

I eye the dress. "That looks familiar. You kept looking at it at one of the boutiques we were at this weekend. But you didn't pick it out."

"Yeah." He grins, holding the dress up to my body. "It's a bit different than the dresses you were going for. But we've been planning on taking you to Evolve ever since Sunday night, and it's perfect for that, so I grabbed it a couple days ago."

My mouth drops. "Evolve? Like, *the* Evolve?"

It's a super exclusive nightclub that I never, ever thought I'd step foot into. And the guys can get in? What the hell?

"Yep. Now get dressed." He hands me the dress, and then he disappears into his bathroom.

I strip, setting my clothes on top of his dresser. Then I pull on the dress. It's a blood red satin slip dress, and it hugs my body perfectly. The cowl neck dips down gracefully, and I brush my fingers against my bare collarbones.

When Oliver comes back into the room, his eyes rake over me with so much heat I squirm. He's put eyeliner on, and I find myself staring at him, because fuck. *Fuck,* he looks good.

Grabbing my hand, Oliver pulls me into the bathroom. There, he does my hair and makeup, peppering my skin with kisses as he does. By the time he's done, the only thing I want to do is strip him bare.

"You look stunning, princess." He turns me around so I can look at myself in the mirror.

He didn't use a lot of makeup, but he painted my lips the exact same shade as my dress. Paired with the earrings and necklace he put on me, I really do look amazing.

"Do you like it?"

"I do. Thank you, Oliver."

His fingers run down my sides, sending a shiver of delight through me. Then with one hand on my lower stomach, he presses my back into his front. The other snakes up my body until his thumb brushes over one of my nipples.

I bite the inside of my lip, suppressing another shiver. But then his lips are on my neck, running downward with a feather-light touch, his breath tickling my skin.

Gripping his arms, a small whimper escapes my mouth. Then he chuckles and pulls away. At the loss of him holding me, I stumble into the counter, grabbing it for balance.

"We should meet the others downstairs. They're probably waiting for us already."

With a groan that he snickers at, I grab my heels, and then we find Rhett and Elliot in the foyer. When they see us, Elliot's jaw drops, and Rhett actually freezes.

After a few seconds of stunned silence, Elliot runs a hand over his hair. "Fuck. You two look entirely too good right now."

I almost suggest we stay in, but Rhett was insistent about me knowing whatever it is I need to know, so I decide against it.

Later. There'll be time later.

Once we're in Elliot's SUV, I take Oliver's hand in the backseat.

There's a certain thrill to not knowing what's about to happen. Normally, it'd make me nervous as hell. But over the past week, my feelings for these men have only deepened. I'd follow them just about anywhere if they asked me to.

I don't think you understand that if, somehow, we lost you, we'd burn the whole world to the fucking ground to find you again.

It's a long drive to the club, but I don't mind. I'm filled with a tingly anticipation at whatever is going to happen tonight. So when we get out of the car and enter the club through a private entrance, I'm so excited that I barely feel the winter air biting at my skin.

Inside, it's loud and overwhelming, with deep purple and blue lights. But Elliot keeps a comforting hand on the small of my back, and Oliver and Rhett stay close as well.

I expect us to head to the bar or the dance floor, but instead Elliot ushers me up a stairwell and into a semi-private room. Through floor-to-ceiling windows, I look down on the dance floor and the ocean of bodies below. You can still hear the music, but it's not as loud.

Standing right behind me, Elliot places his hands on his hips. "Do you know who owns Evolve, Wren?"

I watch his reflection in the window as I shake my head.

"His name is Ludo Holloway. Recognize it?"

I frown. "Maybe? I'm not sure."

Rhett steps up to the window on my right side, and Oliver does the same on my left. The tension rolling off of Rhett is so potent, so intense, that I can't help but reach out and take his hand in mine.

He nods to the floor of the club. "See the sectioned off area? And the man in the red leather jacket?"

It takes me a second, but I find it. The area is slightly raised, overlooking the club. The man Rhett spoke of is slouching on a black couch, arms resting on the back of it with his legs spread open. Two women are sitting on either side of him. He's smirking as he surveys the dance floor, looking like modern-day king.

"I see him."

My stomach sinks. Rhett's expression may be neutral, but the rage rolling off of him tells a different story. I can only think of a couple reasons for it.

When Rhett turns to me, I have to fight not to shrink back from the absolute fury in his eyes.

"He killed my little sister. Sammy."

My breath catches in my throat. It's what I was expecting, but hearing the words out loud still hits hard.

Rhett continues. "Back then, he wasn't nearly as powerful. Now? He owns half of the criminal underworld in the city. There are very few people who don't bow down to him."

"Edgar Williams was one of those people," Elliot says.

What?

Oh my god. No. No, they wouldn't.

"You work for the man who murdered your sister." My voice comes out flat.

"Sometimes, yes."

Pulling away from Elliot, I whip around to face the three of them. "Why? That makes no sense. How can you even stand to look at him? He murdered a child. Your *sister*."

"Because," Rhett says, reaching out and tilting my chin up with a single finger. He doesn't seem phased at all by the disgust in my voice. He just looks down at me with that piercing gaze of his. "The closer we are to him, the better the view of his downfall will be."

He holds my gaze as I put the pieces together.

They aren't just hitmen. Not in the least.

"You're in this for revenge."

Rhett nods.

I blink. Look between the three of them. Then shake my head. "So why the hell is he still alive?"

"It took us years to figure out who killed Sammy. Once we did, we only got a nickname: Redback. From there, we searched to uncover his real identity—which we finally did last year."

Redback. "Like the spider?"

Elliot nods.

"Because he . . ." I grimace.

"Restrains his victims and kills them slowly, just like the spider," Oliver says. "And then he watches them die. Sick fuck likes it."

I shiver. Then my eyes go wide. "Is it safe to talk about this here? What if the room is bugged?"

Rhett shakes his head. "He doesn't bother with rooms like this. There's too much background noise."

I wonder how he knows that for sure, but I don't ask. There are more important questions right now. "And he's not dead because . . . ?"

Elliot takes my hands in his. "He's not dead yet because he deserves worse than that. We're going to utterly destroy him, Wren. After we've completely broken him, *then* we'll kill him."

"Once he's suffered enough," I whisper.

Elliot nods.

It's dark. It's really, *really* dark. But I can't help but think that Ludo Holloway deserves it. How can you kill a child and not hate yourself afterward? How can you find joy in watching an innocent person struggle for their life?

"You have his trust."

"As much as he gives it to anyone. When he wants someone dead but doesn't want to do it himself, he comes to us. We don't always accept, but when we do, we don't fail." Oliver tugs me from Elliot, cupping my cheek with his hand. "I know it's a lot to take in. But you deserve to know the truth. So you know what you're really getting into."

They trust me.

The realization hits as Oliver searches my eyes for any hesitance. This isn't child's play. It isn't trivial or innocent. No, this is what they've made their life's mission—destroy and kill Ludo to get revenge for Sammy.

It's morally gray at best, and highly dangerous and illegal even if it's not. Yet they've revealed it all to me.

My gaze darts between the three of them, and I find that they're all watching me patiently, almost curiously—maybe a little bit hesitantly.

When my eyes lock with Oliver's, I pause for a mere moment. And then I grab his face in my hands and press my lips to his. He lets out a startled sound, but other than that, he doesn't miss a beat. As his arms wrap around my waist, he kisses me back with the same passion that's swelling in my chest.

I pull away first, but only a few inches.

Oliver grins. "It's a good thing I bought you smudge-proof lipstick." Then he's pushing me into Elliot's arms.

"Wren," Elliot murmurs. His thumb runs over my bottom lip.

I don't wait—can't. I kiss him the same way I kissed Oliver, and he keeps pace. It's everything I'm feeling and more. Every shred of affection I have for him. For all of them.

I'm in. I'm in, and I won't betray your trust. I promise.

When I find myself in Rhett's arms, I pause. His expression is pained. Mournful. But there's the happiness that comes along with new beginnings, too. The relief of coming home—or of finding it.

I touch his cheek. His eyes slide shut, and he leans forward, resting his forehead against mine.

"Tell me you understand," he whispers.

"I do. I do, Rhett."

He lets out a shaky breath before capturing my mouth in a kiss. It's all-encompassing. All-consuming. And I'm pretty sure the only things keeping me balanced are his hands on my waist. But then the kiss turns startlingly wet, and I realize my cheeks are coated in tears. *My* tears.

Rhett pulls away, a mixture of concern and fear in his eyes. He's stiff again. "Wren—"

"Oooh. I did *not* use waterproof mascara, princess."

I laugh, but it comes out sounding more like a sob. When Oliver pulls me away from Rhett, I follow until he has me in a ridiculously luxurious bathroom.

"Is this whole thing made of marble?"

"Basically." Tissue in hand, Oliver dabs at my cheeks, and then under my eyes, until he steps back, satisfied. "That'll do, I think. You okay?"

Breathing deeply, I nod. It's a lot to take in. I can't even imagine losing a sibling, let alone dedicating my life to revenge for them. How difficult must it be for them all, especially Rhett, knowing that Ludo is still alive and very much so enjoying his life? At least that's how it looks.

It's disgusting. He doesn't deserve to live.

"Oh my god," I murmur, glancing at my reflection with disbelief.

"What?"

Turning to look at him, I say, "I think I want to kill him, too."

He raises his eyebrows, his lips parting slightly from shock. And then something that looks suspiciously like attraction flashes in his eyes. But as soon as it registers, it's gone.

Looping an arm around my waist, he presses a kiss to my temple. "Let's dance, princess."

Chapter Fourteen

Oliver

Rhett and Elliot stay in the room Holloway always keeps reserved for us. He may think he hides it well, but I know Rhett absolutely detests having any kind of fun when Ludo is around. And considering Sammy got brought up, it's best Elliot stays with him.

But I, personally, am in the mood to celebrate.

We told her. We showed her our deepest, darkest secret, and she didn't shove us away.

As I drag Wren onto the dance floor, I think back over the past week. She's been through so much. And she's handled it beautifully.

I think I want to kill him, too.

When those words spilled out of her mouth, it took everything in me not to fuck her senseless right there. Because it means she gets it. She fucking gets it.

And I couldn't be more relieved.

When we pass by Ludo's spot, I give him a nod. He's still wearing his signature smirk, even more pronounced than usual since one of his top competitors is dead. He tips his head down slightly, his eyes tracking Wren, before he raises an eyebrow at me. With a wink, I turn away, making sure to keep Wren tucked into my side.

Being friendly with your worst enemy is a weird, gut-twisting feeling, but you get used to it eventually. It'll be worth it.

Wren and I fall into the crowd, and soon we're lost in the music and lights. She's been somewhat tense all week, so it's nice to see her let go.

At some point, we get drinks, and I glance up to find Elliot and Rhett watching us. We're safe here, but it's nice to know they have our backs in case there's trouble.

Not that there will be. This place is exclusive for a reason. Ludo Holloway may love violence, but not when he's not in control of it.

"You're about to find out," Wren shouts over the music, "that I'm *very much* a lightweight."

I laugh. "It's okay. I've got you."

Her eyes soften, and she kisses me for a second longer than appropriate before she goes back to dancing.

She seems fine through her first drink. But as she starts sipping her second, it doesn't take long for the alcohol to hit her system. Then she turns into a giggling mess. She can't stop eyeing me, and she gets increasingly handsy. Which I find incredibly cute.

"Impatient, princess?"

She nods enthusiastically, and just as she's about to take another sip of her drink, I ease it out of her hand.

When she protests, I give her an amused look. "Two options, princess. You keep drinking, and we stay until you're ready to pass out. We'll get you home safe and put you to bed."

She pouts.

"*Or* you stop drinking before you're too far gone. I know what you want, Wren. But I'm not going to give it to you if I don't think you're sober enough to consent. Neither will Elliot. Or Rhett."

For a second, she stares at me, and I wonder if she didn't hear me over the music. But then that look crosses her face. It's the one I saw her give us earlier, when we told her we were taking her out but didn't tell her why.

Absolute trust.

She throws her arms around me, pressing a kiss to my jaw. "You're perfect." Then she tilts her head, narrowing her eyes at me. "And really good at eyeliner."

I try not to, but my body goes rigid. It's something I normally wear when we go out, but tonight, the only reason I put it on was because Elliot would've beat my ass bright red if I hadn't.

I would've enjoyed it, but still.

"You don't mind that I'm wearing it?"

She gapes at me. "*Mind* it? Oliver. It's sexy as hell. And it makes me want to kiss you senseless. Mmm. And—and fuck you, too."

I grin. "Soon, princess. For now, let's keep dancing."

After giving me another kiss, she does.

It only takes her a half hour, and then she's seeming much more like herself. Makes sense, considering she didn't have that much alcohol.

Still, I don't want to rush things.

I lean in, my lips brushing against her ear, smiling to myself when she melts at the light touch. "I'm going to get you some water."

With a quick glance to make sure Elliot and Rhett are watching her, I leave her and grab a cup of water. As I'm making my way back over to her, I notice Ludo staring in her direction.

No, not in her direction. *At her.*

The heated interest in his eyes has my stomach roiling with disgust. He doesn't even deserve to be in the same room as her. My steps quicken, and I have to avert my eyes before someone catches me giving Ludo a scathing glare.

I'm not possessive. Really, I'm not.

Okay, maybe I am. A little.

Because when I get back to Wren, I don't hand her the water. Instead, I wrap an arm around her waist and pull her into me. Her hands are instantly on my chest, grabbing at my shirt, as I seal my lips to hers in a... yeah. It's a possessive damn kiss, and I don't fucking care. Ludo can keep his hands—and his eyes—to himself.

"Oliver," she gasps when I finally release her.

Handing her the water, I lean in close. "Drink up."

She takes the cup and gulps half of it down.

"Good girl."

She practically glows at my praise.

We stick to the dance floor for a couple more minutes. The entire time, I keep my hands on her in some capacity. The way her body moves against mine is intoxicating, and I also want to make sure Ludo knows his fucking place: far away from Wren.

Eventually, I grab her hand and tug. She follows me without question, and I pull her into a deserted back hallway. Once we're around a corner and out of sight, I pin her to the wall and capture her mouth with mine.

Her fingers thread into my hair as she tries to get as close to me as possible. Considering the desperation that's been building up in her ever since I teased her at home, she'd probably let me strip her down right here.

Not that I would.

Her hand slips under the front of my shirt, and I groan into her mouth. It only eggs her on, and as our kiss deepens, her hips roll into mine slowly.

When I pull away, her eyes are unfocused and heavy-lidded, and her breaths are coming out in short pants.

"I'm sober enough, Oliver. I promise."

Tracing the outline of her jaw, I say, "And impatient."

She lets out an adorable little whine.

My hands drop to her thighs, playing with the hem of her dress. Then I trail them upward, painfully slowly, until they're tracing her breasts. When my fingers reach her collarbones, her head falls back against the wall.

"Maybe I should just do this for a while. See how worked up I can get you." To be honest, I'm not sure how much patience *I* have left. But she doesn't know that.

She whimpers, and one of her hands reaches to pull her dress up. I snatch it away.

"Oliver!"

"You can touch me, princess. And I'll touch you."

Her eyes flare all the way open. And then, slowly, she places both hands on my chest. Her fingers travel lightly, tracing the curves and edges of my body. My jawbone, my cheeks, my neck. My arms, my shoulders, my stomach. With every tiny touch, she sends tendrils of warmth and pleasure through me.

When her hands reach my hips, she glances up at me questioningly. I nod. "Go on."

Her fingers brush downward, grazing my cock. At the same time, I let my hands cup her breasts. My thumbnails run over her nipples through her dress.

"*Ohhh.*"

"Don't stop, Wren." I repeat the action, staring at the way her nipples peak perfectly through the red fabric.

Her fingers wrap around my dick the best they can through my pants, and she strokes it in up and down motions. For a few blissful seconds, the noises of the club fade away, and the only thing that exists is us.

But then a shrill, female laugh cuts through the air, too close for comfort. Wren tenses.

I pause, listening for footsteps, but no one rounds the corner. When I step back, Wren grabs my arms.

"Please don't stop."

When I look at her, I see a little thrill in her eyes. "Does the thought of getting caught excite you, princess?"

She bites her lip and avoids my gaze, staring at my chest instead.

"I'll take that as a yes." Taking her hand, I place it back on my dick. Then, with a small kiss, I pinch her nipples.

Her back arches, and her grip on my cock tightens.

"Tell me what you want, Wren." I nip at her ear before groaning. Her hand feels so goddamned good.

"I want your fingers," she whispers. "Inside of me. I'm off my period."

"Mmm. I'd do it either way, princess. Do you want me to make you come?"

She nods.

One of my hands stays on her breast, tweaking her nipple, while the other falls in between her legs, pushing her dress up slightly. When I push her thong to the side, her free hand comes up to grip the back of my neck.

She's so wet she's practically dripping. "So needy," I murmur smugly in her ear. Then I slip a single finger inside of her.

"More," she moans.

I oblige, adding another and curling them into her. She whimpers, her strokes slowing from distraction.

"Don't slow down, Wren, or I will too."

She gasps, picking up her pace again.

"Just like that." I run my tongue across her bottom lip before kissing her. When she opens her mouth, I slide my tongue inside, meeting hers. She tastes like the sugary, fruity drink she had, and I can't get enough.

"Oliver," she says, breaking away after a minute. "Use your thumb on my clit."

Grinning, I do. I knew she wanted it, but I wanted her to tell me to do it. I love hearing her beg, but having her command me to do something? Ten times better.

"Fuck," she whispers. Her eyes slide closed, and I half expect her hand to slow down again, but it doesn't.

"Look at you," I say lowly in her ear. "Don't even have enough patience to wait until we get home. You're going to let me fuck you right here, aren't you?"

Her breath hitches, and she nods.

"You know what that makes you?" I nip at her bottom lip, still curling my fingers into her and rubbing her clit with my thumb. "A filthy slut. Doesn't it?"

"Yes. I am—ohhh god."

I smile to myself. Rhett can't stand being degraded, but Elliot likes it. And watching Wren melt at my words is just as fun as watching him do the same.

She stretches upward, capturing my lips in a desperate, clumsy kiss. When I pick up the pace of my fingers, she moans, doing the same with her hand on my dick.

The tension, the anticipation, the fear of getting caught—it all drives me into a lustful haze. My mouth waters at the thought of tasting her. Of having my tongue inside of her.

Pinching her nipple one last time, I say, "Do you want me to use my mouth on you?"

"God yes. Please. *Please.*"

"Order me to do it, princess."

There's an infinitesimal moment of hesitance, but then she smiles. "Get on your knees, Oliver. Now."

I do, resting both hands on her thighs and looking up at her. Waiting.

It takes her a second to catch on. Then, with a nervous giggle, she shifts her weight to one leg. "Put my leg over your shoulder."

When I do, I kiss her inner thigh, and I realize she's quivering with excitement. *Me too, princess.*

"I want your fingers still inside of me. And then use your tongue and your mouth on my clit."

I groan. "With pleasure."

Then I dive in. With two fingers moving in and out of her, I tease her clit with my tongue, relishing in the way she tastes. I can't help the grunt of appreciation that leaves my throat.

"Harder, Oliver. You've teased me enough."

I chuckle, nuzzling my face against her, before obeying. When I press small circles to her clit with my tongue, her knee almost gives out. I grab her hip with my free hand to steady her, pulling away for a second.

"Use the wall for balance."

She leans into it, panting, and I go back to using my tongue on her. My fingers move in and out of her, hitting one of her sensitive spots. Her tiny moans and whimpers have my cock so hard, it's straining painfully against my pants.

I'd say I regret getting on my knees instead of going straight to fucking her, but I don't. I'll always enjoy eating her out.

And, my god, I'm going to do whatever is necessary to make sure there is a forever.

"Oliver," she gasps. "Oliver, I'm going to come. It feels too good."

And then she's biting her hand so she doesn't scream, her eyes rolling back into her head, as her orgasm washes over her. It's a beautiful sight. Mesmerizing, even.

As she comes down, I slowly pull my fingers from her. Then I slide her leg off my shoulder, because she's so dazed it looks like she might fall over.

When I stand up, she doesn't even give me a split second before her arms are wrapped around my neck and she's kissing me. She moans at her taste on my tongue, or maybe it's because of the way I press her into the wall with my body.

I don't care. All that matters is that I have her. *We* have her.

"Do you want me to fuck you?"

"I *need* you to fuck me."

With a smirk, I wrap an arm around her waist. "Come with me."

It's too out in the open for what I want to do. I don't want to have to be listening for people coming down the hallway the whole time.

I scan each of the doors we pass. Most are offices, then there are bathrooms for the staff, and then—perfect.

Dragging her through the door labeled "Maintenance," I give the room a once-over. Empty except for shelves of cleaning supplies, toilet paper, and the works. And in the far corner, a table that's exactly the height I'm looking for.

I lead her over to it, and then I yank her dress up, exposing her ass. She gasps, glancing at the door, but she doesn't look too worried.

"This okay?"

"Yes."

"Good," I murmur. Then I pick her up and set her on the table. It's not very big, so her shoulder blades hit the wall behind it when I lift her legs, placing them on my shoulders.

She lets out a surprised squeak, probably from effectively being folded in half. I run a finger down her legs, then over her clit, and she jumps.

"You ready?"

With a nod, she reaches for my pants, but I beat her to it. I shove them down with my boxers, and instantly her gaze is fixated on my cock and the way I'm pumping it with my hand.

I line myself up with her entrance, but then I stop. "Hold on to me."

One of her hands wraps around my neck, her fingers twisting into my hair. She keeps the other on the table, gripping the edge.

Then I slide into her, kissing her bare calf as I do. I'm already drunk off of her—her taste, her smell, the way she can't stop shaking. But when a little "*Fuck*," comes out of her mouth, it takes every ounce of my willpower to keep my pace slow.

She meets my thrusts with her own attempts, but one of her legs begins to slip off my shoulder. I grab it, putting it back in place and holding it there. She tries again, but I shake my head, leaning down and kissing her.

"Let me, princess. You can touch yourself. I want to feel you come around my dick."

Her eyes flutter closed for a second. Then, eyes locked on mine, she uses her middle finger to circle her clit.

"That's it," I say, watching her, never wanting to look away. My self-control runs out, and my thrusts quicken. When Wren's moans get louder, pride unfurls in my chest.

"It's a good thing Elliot can't see you," I chide playfully. "He'd be trying to make you scream right now."

She bites her lip to try to muffle her moans.

This entire time, she hasn't looked away from me, and it's made the whole thing so much more intense. When she clenches around me, I groan. She feels so warm, so right, so fucking perfect.

She's not going to be able to hold on for long.

Shit. I don't think I'll be able to, either.

I slow down. This is just the beginning of a long night of exploring each other's bodies, but I don't want this part to end. The four of us all together is indescribable, but this? Being alone with any of them, having their body all to myself, being the center of their attention?

That's its own kind of heaven.

"Oliver," Wren moans. "I'm so close."

I lean forward, pressing her legs even closer into her body, and slam into her. She cries out, forgetting to stay quiet, and I smirk before my mouth meets hers.

The way her lips move against mine is unfocused and unsteady. And then she's not kissing me at all, instead whispering, "Oh god, oh god oh god oh *fuck*."

It's one of the hottest things I've ever witnessed.

I pull away ever so slightly, watching as her back arches and her face goes slack with ecstasy. The way she feels as she comes on my cock is pulling me closer to the edge, and I'm trying to hold on, but fuck. How am I supposed to when it all feels so good?

With a shuddering breath, I slow my thrusts, trying to draw out her orgasm and delay my own. It seems to work, because she lets out something like a sob, and her middle finger is still moving on her clit with a feather-light touch.

When she whimpers again, I clap a hand over her mouth.

"Those noises, Wren. They're going to make me come. And I'm not ready yet, dammit."

She grunts against my hand, then takes in a series of short breaths through her nose. Only when her hand falls away from her clit do I release her.

"Holy shit," she says, the words coming out all tired and breathy. Her eyes are closed, her hair is a bit of a mess, and she looks absolutely ravaged.

Well, not *absolutely*. That's how she'll look when Rhett and Elliot are through with her. But I'm proud of my part in it.

Wren grips the table with one hand, and with the other she runs her hand lightly over my chest. One of her fingers brushes over my nipple, and the zap of electricity it sends through me has me swearing.

"Oh my god," she murmurs. She does it again, and I grip her legs tighter. My hips pick up their speed without my permission. The feeling is too addictive.

Just like I did to her earlier, Wren uses her thumbnail to lightly scrape my nipple through my shirt. She doesn't stop, watching me with rapt fascination.

"Wren," I groan. *Not yet. Fuck, not yet.*

But my body betrays me, my vision blacking out as I finish. Wren rubs my nipple one last time before she's pulling me down and kissing me. All of this barely registers in my mind as I come, wave after wave of pleasure overwhelming me. When I'm finally able to think again, it hits me that I'm not kissing her back, too lost in the euphoria.

We break off the kiss and stare at each other, chests heaving and hearts pounding. Gently, I lower her legs and pull her into a tight embrace. When I release her, there's so much emotion on her face that it should probably terrify me.

It doesn't.

I kiss her. "Come on, princess. We should get back before Ell and Rhett get too jealous."

Besides, I have a plan I need to set in motion.

Chapter Fifteen

Rhett

When Oliver texts me, my body floods with relief. In minutes, Elliot and I are downstairs by the private entrance we came in through. I spot Oliver and Wren, and I have to hold back a laugh.

They're both wrecked. Hell, they look like two teenagers at prom who just fucked in the bathroom.

When we get to the SUV, I'm so happy to be putting distance in between myself and Ludo that I don't even care when Oliver and Wren push me into the backseat. Or that they put *me*, the biggest out of all of us, in the middle seat.

Before she gets in the car, Wren pins Elliot against his door and kisses him. To say he's taken by surprise would be an understatement. But he kisses her back with as much enthusiasm as she gives.

Inside, he couldn't take his eyes off her and Oliver. And god, neither could I. The way they were dancing together was so fucking hot it hurt.

"She'd better be sober," I say darkly in Oliver's ear. On the dance floor earlier, I saw him take Wren's drink away, but she was definitely acting tipsy.

He just kisses me. "You know I wouldn't do anything if she wasn't."

As he takes me in, his expression softens. My skin is already crawling—always does when I'm around Ludo—and it doesn't go away when Oliver reaches out and brushes his fingers over my cheek. But my heart warms all the same.

I need you, Oliver. And I'm sorry I can't be what you need.

"Are you okay?"

"That's the last thing I want to talk about right now, O."

Understanding flickers over his features, along with something that looks uncomfortably like pity. It disappears quickly. He knows what'll happen if he presses further, and it's not what any of us want right now.

So I take his face in my hands, bringing my lips within an inch of his. For a moment, I hesitate, giving him a chance to pull away if he wants to. But he closes the distance instead.

With a groan, I hold his head still, devouring him. The faint tang of alcohol is mixed with Wren's taste, and I swipe my tongue over his, trying to get more of it.

Oliver lets me ravage his mouth, turning pliant in my arms. I've missed him. I've been keeping my distance, not wanting to accidentally trigger him into another panic attack. Elliot and Wren are both more stable, and much more capable of helping him through one. The only thing I can do is try to get him to breathe deeply, and sometimes I freeze up before I can even do that.

But this? Kissing him—*devouring* him? That I can do. And it's nice to have a couple seconds alone without feeling like I'm going to accidentally harm him.

Just as Oliver is about to turn into a literal puddle, a gust of cold air rushes in. I turn, looking behind me to find the door open. Wren is standing there, breathless from kissing Elliot. She's staring at us with a look of enraptured awe on her pretty face.

"Get in, sweetheart, before you freeze."

That seems to snap her out of her stupor. She climbs in, shutting the door behind her, before she exchanges a mischievous grin with Oliver.

What the hell is that about?

I release Oliver and run a hand over Wren's hair. Then I wrap my hand around her throat. She watches me with a lidded gaze as a smile spreads over her face. Her head tilts back slightly, giving my hand more room.

I can't help but chuckle to myself at what a mess she is. Her hair isn't nearly as neat as it was when we left home, and the smear-proof lipstick Oliver put on her is *definitely* smudged a bit.

What I really care about, though, is that the tears that were in her eyes earlier are gone. Not that I won't put more in them tonight. But those will be a different kind—the best kind.

"This is entirely unfair," Elliot grouses from the driver's seat. He's turned on the car and is just beginning to pull out of our parking spot.

"You'll get your turn," I tell him, laughing when he glares at me in the rearview mirror.

Then I turn to Wren, only to find her with that fascinated look in her eyes again.

"What?"

"Your laugh," she murmurs, tracing my face with her fingers. "It's really nice."

Fuck. I know I don't laugh a lot. It just . . . doesn't happen. But I didn't realize this is the first time she's seen it. I mean, I suppose she's seen a chuckle or an amused look here and there, but—yeah. I think this really is the first time she's seen it.

"Rhett," she whispers, her gaze fixed on my mouth. "Can I kiss you?"

Gathering her up in my arms, I press my lips to hers. But then she's squirming away, grabbing one of my arms and tugging it off of her. At first, I'm confused, but then she places my hand so it's wrapped around her throat again.

I raise an eyebrow, expecting her to look away shyly, but she doesn't.

"It makes me feel like I'm y-" She cuts herself off, then shakes her head like she's trying to get a thought out of her head.

I barely have time to think about what she was about to say. She kisses me so desperately, so brazenly, it becomes the only thing I can focus on. She tastes sweet. So sweet.

When I squeeze her neck lightly, she moans, gripping my shoulders. It's a similar reaction to the one Oliver has when I do that to him. As if on cue, I hear him groaning behind me.

After a few seconds, Wren pulls away, glancing at Oliver. "It's his turn now." She gives me one last peck.

Then I'm being tugged in the other direction, and I turn to face Oliver. He's on me before I can make a comment about how these two are acting like they *didn't* just fuck.

Just as I wrap my hand around Oliver's throat, relishing in the groan that it rips from him, I feel a hand trailing up my thigh. Wren rubs my dick through my pants, and I find myself involuntarily grinding into her.

Then she leans down, pressing a kiss to my cock before licking the fabric above it.

"Fuck," I hiss. "Did you two plan this?"

"Maybe," Wren says with a giggle. Then she's spreading my legs and somehow squeezing onto the floor in front of me. There's not a lot of room, but she makes it work.

"Devious," I mutter. I'm not able to say much more, because Oliver's mouth is already on mine again.

This man knows how to plan a good distraction.

Wren fumbles with the button and zipper of my pants for a minute before she reaches in, pulling my boxers away, and unleashes my cock. She actually moans at the sight of it, and then her tongue darts out, circling the tip.

My mind goes blank for a second, and Oliver takes the opportunity to pull my shirt up. His hand splays across my hot skin, and he gains control of the kiss, his other hand gripping my hair so he can maneuver my head however he wants.

He's trying to keep my mind off Holloway, so I let him stay in control for a few seconds. Then I squeeze his throat and nip lightly at his bottom lip, and just like that he's melting, his hand in my hair loosening.

Wren's lips close around my cock. One of her hands encircles it, moving up and down in time with her mouth, while the other rests on my thigh. I have to fight to stay present, to not lose myself in the feeling.

Shit, she feels good.

Gripping Oliver's jaw, I pull away from him. He opens his mouth without me even having to tell him.

"You want my spit, do you?"

He nods, closing his eyes in lustful, needy anticipation. When I spit into his mouth, he swallows with a satisfied smile.

Then I realize that Wren's mouth isn't on my dick anymore. We both look down, and we're met with that captivated, curious expression yet again.

"You want some too, little slut?"

She nods.

"Then be a good girl and take it."

She doesn't even hesitate. Her mouth opens, and she sits up, stretching toward me. I lean down, taking hold of her jaw, before I spit into her mouth.

"Now use it on my cock."

She obeys immediately, licking the underside of my dick before resuming her previous pace.

"Fuck all of you," Elliot groans.

"Oh you will, pretty boy," I say smoothly.

He lets out a frustrated noise, his fingers tapping on the steering wheel. We're used to the long drive in and out of the city, but this must be fucking torture for him.

We'll make it worth his wait.

I go back to making out with Oliver, holding him in place while I shove my tongue down his throat. He eats it up like I knew he would.

"When we get home, you're fucking mine, O," I say.

"On one condition." He leans in, murmuring in my ear, "You stop *fucking* avoiding me."

I freeze. When he pulls away, I search his face. Mostly, his stare is challenging. But there, hiding behind the bit of anger, is the hurt.

"I—"

I don't want to make things worse.

I don't want to remind you of how scared you were.

I don't know how to help you.

"I'm not fragile, Rhett," he says quietly enough that only I hear.

He's not. I know he's not. He's one of the bravest people I know. Hell, just a week ago, he was jumping into the line of fire to keep me safe.

But that's the thing, isn't it? He did it because he was scared of losing me. And since that night when he thought he lost us, every time I look at him, his eyes are still a little haunted.

"Oliver . . ."

His gaze hardens. He's not going to back down. "I'll be okay. Now say it, Rhett."

I blow out a breath. "I'll stop avoiding you. I'm sorry."

Tugging on the hand still wrapped around his throat, Oliver presses his lips to my palm. It's a tender action, one that makes my heart beat a thousand times faster.

"I love you," he says, gently yet forcefully. And then he kisses me before I have a chance to reply, like he knows how easily I choke on those words.

Because he does.

I hold his head in my hands, silently promising to do better. Over the years, I've improved, but my god do I still have a long way to go.

Wren changes up what she's doing, focusing on the tip of my cock and sucking. Her tongue runs along the underside every time she moves up and down, right where it's sensitive, and I grunt into Oliver's mouth.

The way he kisses me changes, and this time, when he fights for control, I give it freely.

There isn't a thing I wouldn't *give you, O.*

I let him taste me, let him shove his tongue down my throat like I did to him earlier. And maybe it's messy, but it's what I like. At the same time, Wren starts sucking my cock harder. I swear, they're coordinating with each other.

When Oliver gives me a chance to breathe, I say with a strained voice, "You're going to make me come in your mouth, sweetheart."

Wren moans, the motions of her hand and mouth becoming more enthusiastic, like that's exactly what she *wants* me to do.

Fuck, this woman.

"Rhett," Oliver groans, and I realize—like an absolute idiot—that he's missed me, too. That, possibly, he didn't drag me into the backseat with Wren just to distract me from Holloway. It was to corner me, so I'd be forced to fix things.

And then I'm done letting Oliver have control. I take back the kiss fiercely, gripping his throat. My mouth moves against his so forcefully that it pushes him backward, and I have to hold the back of his head to keep him steady. He takes every bruising, branding kiss, matching my desperation with his own.

"Fuck," Elliot mutters.

Oliver and I give him a glance. We're sitting at a red light, and he's looking back at the three of us. His eyes are pure fire, and I'd bet a large sum of money that his cock is rock hard right now.

His gaze rakes over me, hot and lustful.

I think that's what does me in. The want in his eyes, and the fact that he's watching. I barely have time to give Wren a warning before I'm spurting into her mouth. I let it take me under, let Oliver capture every one of my moans with his mouth.

Wren's grip on me loosens, and when my cock drops from her mouth, she sticks out her tongue so I can see my cum coating it.

"Fuck. *Fuck*."

We all jump when the car behind us honks their horn.

"Shit," Elliot says, turning back around and hitting the gas. The light's green now.

Wren swallows my cum, then she rests her head against my thigh, gazing up at me with a radiant look on her face.

"Get up here."

As soon as she's within my reach, I haul her into my arms, and then I drop her onto mine and Oliver's lap. She's on her stomach, her head inches from Oliver's crotch, with her torso spread over my legs.

Pulling up her dress, I squeeze her ass, and she moans. Then I flip her over, and she squeals from surprise.

"If you make her come, I'm going to get us into a fucking car crash," Elliot practically growls.

"Noooo!" Wren whines. "Please don't tease me again. *Please*."

"I said it the other day, and I'll say it again, princess. We need to work on your self-preservation instincts."

I have no idea what Oliver is talking about, but the scowl Wren gives him is amusing and cute as hell.

I trace a finger down her exposed stomach, following her thong. She's absolutely soaked.

"I don't think fuckdolls get a say in what happens to them. What do you think, Oliver?"

"Sounds about right to me."

Wren huffs. But then her face breaks out into a smile, even as she says, "You two are the worst."

Tracing her collarbones, Oliver grins down at her. Then he's pushing the straps of her dress down until she threads her arms through them. Once the red fabric is bunched around her waist, his fingers run over the soft skin of her breasts. She whimpers when he refuses to touch her nipples.

I do something similar, pushing her thong to the side. But I don't touch her clit. Instead, with a feather-light touch, I run my fingers through her labia and gently circle the outside of her vagina, touching her everywhere except where she wants.

Her whimpers turn more desperate. When she reaches for my hand, trying to push it to where she wants, I take both of her wrists and hold them for Oliver to grab. He does, pinning them to his chest. Wren groans, trying to pull free, but his grip is too strong.

"You three will be the death of me," she mutters.

Oliver snickers, finally letting a finger graze one of her nipples. She swears, her back arching. Unconsciously, she parts her legs until one of them falls off the seat.

Seeing her splayed out for us like a feast has me getting hard again already. I trace her entrance one more time before slipping two fingers inside of her. She gasps, wriggling her hips to get them further inside, so I pull them almost all the way out.

I do that for a while, sliding in and out of her, not trying to hit any of her sensitive spots, and not using enough fingers to make her feel full. Oliver keeps teasing her breasts, only touching her nipples now and then.

When I finally circle her clit, her moan is so loud and so long, you'd think she was in pain if you didn't know the situation she's in.

"Don't you dare stop," she gasps.

"What did I say about fuckdolls, Wren?"

She whines, grinding against my fingers, so I pull them away completely. Then she pouts, clenching her fists against Oliver's chest.

"Can you be a good girl, Wren? Can you take what I give you?"

Her chest is heaving, and she's trembling in my lap. "I—I can."

My finger returns to her clit, stroking gently. "You're going to regret saying that, sweetheart."

She looks to Oliver for help, but he shrugs.

With my free hand, I slowly slide three fingers into her, still working her clit with the other. She gasps at the feeling, no doubt expecting that I'd keep teasing her.

But no, I have something else in mind.

The first time I bring her right to the edge, I wonder if she thinks I forgot what Elliot said. But right before she comes, I stop.

"Rhett," she sobs, craning her neck to look at me. "Please."

"You said you'd be good, sweetheart."

Her head falls into Oliver's lap, and he strokes his hand down her cheek. I give her another minute before I start working her again, circling her clit and curling my fingers into her.

She tries to quiet her moans to hide her impending orgasm, but I feel her clench around me, and when she grabs onto Oliver's shirt, I stop again.

"Oh my god," she pants. "I'm going to *die*."

"So dramatic," I say, my tone amused and demeaning.

Just like before, I give her a minute before starting up again. She glares at me, but soon she's whimpering and moaning, trying desperately not to squirm.

"Don't try to hide your orgasm again, or you'll be in a shit ton of trouble," Oliver tells her. "Trust me—I know from experience."

She takes his advice, and when the noises she's making get more frequent, I ease out of her and still my finger on her clit.

She doesn't try to protest this time, just melts into us.

Then the lighting changes. We all look up, and I realize Elliot is pulling into the garage.

We're home.

"My room," Elliot says, slamming the car into park. "Fucking *now*."

I help Wren put her dress back on, and then she's sliding out of the SUV. Her feet barely hit the floor before Elliot grabs her and throws her over his shoulder.

She yelps, but then she laughs, grabbing onto the back of his shirt.

Before we make it out of the garage, I grab Oliver's hand, and we follow Elliot and Wren upstairs, just like that.

In Elliot's room, he throws Wren onto the bed. I expect him to start fucking her immediately, but instead he kneels by her legs, undoing her heels and gently sliding them off her feet. Her eyes are still wild from deprivation, but her demeanor softens at the gesture.

"Elliot," she whispers.

"Do you have any idea how fucking *sexy* your moans sounded in the car?" He kisses her inner thighs. "My mouth was practically watering just from listening to you, Wren."

She runs her fingers through her hair. "You wouldn't let me come."

"It was already distracting enough, love." His fingers run up her thigh, hooking around her thong. "Up."

She leans back on her arms, lifting her ass so he can slide the tiny panties down her legs.

Bringing the thong to his nose, he inhales deeply, groaning. "I could smell you the entire drive home. Do you want to know what that did to me?"

She nods silently.

"It drove me mad, Wren. Absolutely mad." He stands, reaching behind her and unzipping her dress. Then he pulls it over her head, leaving her naked and exposed. "I want to take my time with you, love. But I'm going to fuck you first. That drive was too goddamned long."

I pull Oliver into me, and he looks up at me expectantly. "Do you want to watch, or do you want me to get started on you *while* you watch?"

"Just watch," he murmurs. Then he turns to face the bed, pulling my arms so they wrap around his waist from behind. He leans into me with a sigh.

Elliot flips Wren onto her stomach, pulling her so her ass is up in the air but her head is pressed into the mattress. She's right on the edge of the bed, and we have a perfect view of just how wet she is.

Elliot has his pants undone in record time. He steps up to her, stroking her ass. "You ready, love?"

"If you wait one more second, I will literally, *actually* die, Elliot."

He laughs, sliding into her, and she moans. Not even bothering to go slowly this time around, he grabs her hips, slamming into her repeatedly. She meets each of his thrusts with one of her own, and she's so sensitive that she comes in under a minute, screaming into the mattress.

"Fuck," Oliver says under his breath.

I tighten my hold on him with one arm, letting the other wander up his body until it meets his neck. I don't grab it, just stroke his pulse point with my thumb.

I'm not normally this cuddly, especially during sex, but if it's what Oliver wants from me, it's what he's getting. It already kills me that I hurt him.

That's not what I was trying to do. I promise.

One of Wren's hands snakes in between her legs as Elliot pounds into her from behind. She looks lost in a pleasure-filled world of her own, and when her finger finds her clit, she lets out a muffled cry into the blankets.

"Muffle your screams one more time, and I'll make you regret it."

"How many times do you think we can make her come tonight?" Oliver whispers.

"I'm willing to find out. How many times did she come when she was with you?"

"Two. So that was her third."

"Do you want two of us to fill you at the same time, love?"

"Please," she whimpers.

I grab the lube from his nightstand and hand it to him before returning to Oliver. Ell takes no time getting the lube onto a finger and smearing it over her tight little hole.

"Deep breaths, love," Elliot says.

She gasps them in, her eyes falling closed. It doesn't take too long to prep her, considering she's already fucked into relaxation. By the time Elliot has three fingers in her, all while he's still fucking her, she's barely holding on for dear life.

"Oh my god," Oliver says to me. "She's going to come *again*."

We watch as she falls apart, screaming Elliot's name. After all the teasing and edging we did to her, she must be so sensitive. Which is exactly what I wanted.

Slowing, Elliot leans over her body, stroking her hair. She whimpers when he kisses her shoulder, murmuring something in her ear.

Oliver turns in my arms so he's looking up at me. "Finish up with her before you start with me. I have no desire to be toyed with." He purses his lips. "Well, teased, at least."

I narrow my eyes at him.

"I'm still all yours tonight," he says, kissing my jaw and then my neck. "Elliot knows. And so does Wren. But I didn't put that mascara on her for nothing."

"I didn't miss that," I murmur in his ear.

"You're welcome." He nudges me toward the bed.

After stripping, I climb on, settling on the edge with my legs hanging off. Elliot thrusts into Wren a few more times before pulling out.

"Go to him," he says, grabbing the lube again.

Slowly, she does. Her entire body is trembling, and after she straddles me and sinks down onto my cock, she rests her head on my shoulder. *Hmm.* She might be farther gone than I thought.

"Are you going to be able to handle more after this?" I say, stroking her back and pressing a kiss to her hair.

She nods. "Don't want to stop. Might need a break. But not my mouth. I . . . I want you to use me, Rhett. Please?"

"Oh, trust me, sweetheart. By the end of the night, you'll be so thoroughly fucked that you won't even be able to walk. You'll be a boneless, whimpering, used-up mess. That's a promise."

She gasps in a tiny breath, pulling back to look at me. Considering how tired she is right now, I'm sure she can't imagine feeling like even *more* of a mess.

But if Oliver and I have anything to say about it, she will.

"That's what you want? To be our obedient little whore?"

She smiles, nodding.

"Good. Because Oliver and I have a little game going. We want to see how many times we can make you come tonight. I, for one, am pretty curious."

"Oh my god," she whispers. "But women—women can come a *lot*." Her hesitancy is contradicted by the way she starts grinding against me.

"I'm well aware, sweetheart." With a short kiss, I say, "If you need us to stop, you tell us, okay?"

"Okay." She relaxes, resting her forehead against mine as she rides me. It feels good. Too good, considering I'm saving my cum for someone else tonight.

Elliot comes up behind Wren, stepping in between my legs. "Lay back."

I do, pulling Wren with me, giving Elliot access to her ass. He fingers her a little bit more before pressing his lubed-up cock into her.

It's just an inch or so, but Wren whimpers. Then she takes a couple deep breaths. Her hands are splayed across my chest, her body pressed to mine, and I can feel her heart beating wildly.

Ell slides in more, and I groan at the feeling of him, only separated by a thin wall. I thrust up into Wren, and he grunts.

"Oh god."

It's Wren who says it, her fingers digging into my pecs. I do it again, in time with Elliot, and her eyes roll into the back of her head.

Then Elliot fists her hair, pulling, and I help push her up. He doesn't let go, instead holding it as he fucks her ass. I pick up my pace, too, grabbing her wrists and holding them.

I love seeing her like this—helpless, only held up by us, and completely fucked to oblivion. It's beautiful.

Keeping her wrists restrained with one of my hands, I reach down and flick her clit with the other. She cries out, her body jerking, so Elliot wraps an arm around her waist to hold her still.

She clenches around me when I massage circles into her clit, and I groan. She feels so warm and tight with us both filling her, and the sensations of Elliot rubbing against my dick are heavenly.

"How does it feel?" Elliot says, letting go of her hair and gripping her chin instead. He turns her head so she's looking at him. "Being fucked like this? Only sluts let two people fill them at once."

"Perfect," she whispers. "It feels perfect."

He kisses her, and it's demanding and hard, dominating and controlling. There isn't a single thing she can do, since he's holding her there and I've trapped her wrists. And if the way she practically dissolves into the kiss is any indication, she loves it.

Oliver is similar in a lot of ways. Take away his control, and that's when he feels the most free. *Euphoric*—that's how he describes it.

When I look over at him, he has a greedy look in his eyes.

"You wish this was you?"

He scowls and flips me off.

"Wren. Fuck," Elliot grits out. Then he slams his lips to hers as he comes, holding onto her like she's his lifeline.

It pushes her over the edge, too, and I groan at the feeling of them both coming. Thank fuck neither of them lasted long.

Elliot lets Wren down gently, and I release her wrists so she can hold herself up. Once I'm sitting up, I lift her off my cock, and then Elliot crawls on the bed and pulls her onto his lap. She leans her head against his chest while she tries to catch her breath.

"That was five," I say, pushing her hair out of her face.

Elliot frowns. "Five what?"

"Orgasms." I smirk. "Oliver and I want to see how many times we can make her come."

Elliot's chest shakes with silent laughter as he stares down at the limp woman in his arms. "You sure she can take more?"

She perks up then. "Yes. I can."

"Good," Elliot murmurs, kissing the tip of her nose. "Because I'm not done with you. And I don't think Rhett is either."

Chapter Sixteen

Elliot

Wren sinks into me, smiling. "Yes, please."

I stroke her back, glancing at Rhett. "Do you want me to tie her up?"

"Hands behind her back," he tells me. "I want her helpless."

Wren inhales a shuddering breath, squirming in my lap.

"What do you think about that, love?"

"You can do anything to me," she whispers. "I trust you."

Fuck me.

Gently, I ease her onto the bed so she's laying on her stomach. Then I grab some of my ropes and pull her hands behind her back.

"Tell me if I make them too tight, Wren."

As I loop the ropes around her wrists, she sighs happily, like she's been waiting for this all day. Maybe she has. I pull the ropes tight enough that she won't be able to get free, but loose enough that they won't cut off her blood circulation.

When I'm finished, I pull her up into a sitting position. "How do they feel?"

She tests them, wiggling a bit. "Good."

"You're ready for more? Or do you need another minute?"

Her gaze meets Rhett's, heated and curious. "I'm good."

"Then get on your knees."

She's about to get up, but he doesn't really give her a chance. He grabs her, hauling her off the bed and onto the floor. When he forces her to her knees, she yelps in surprise, but when she looks up at him, excitement flashes in her eyes.

Oliver grabs a glass of water that's on the dresser. He must've gotten it while Rhett and I were fucking Wren. Crouching in front of her, he presses the glass to her lips, and she takes a sip. I head into the bathroom, washing my hands, and when I come back out, Oliver is handing the half-empty water glass to Rhett.

"Do you want to know why I didn't use waterproof mascara on you, princess?" Oliver asks, running his fingers down the bare skin of her arms.

"Because you didn't have any?" she says, voice trembling.

"Oh, no, princess. It's because Rhett loves making a mess of whoever he's fucking. He's going to have tears and makeup and drool streaming down your face by the time he's done with you. And you're going to love it."

Her reaction is perfect. A hint of nervousness, mixed with the thrill of surrendering herself to another person.

Rhett steps in front of her. "If you need a break, open and close your hands. Elliot will watch you. How does that sound?"

She tries it out, seeing how much room she has to move her hands around. Then she nods.

"Your mouth felt so good earlier, sweetheart. But I'm not going to let you have control this time. You want to be used? I'm going to show you exactly what that means."

He grips her jaw, forcing it open, before he leans down and spits in her mouth. She swallows it greedily.

"Such a good girl," he says, and she beams at his words. Then he drags his cock over her bottom lip. "You don't get any more of my cum, though. That's for Oliver."

From where he's leaning against my dresser, Oliver grins. He's been waiting patiently, enjoying the show, getting more and more eager by the second.

Wren gags. When I look back, Rhett is holding her hair—which is now completely ruined—with his dick shoved all the way down her throat. He holds her there while she chokes, smiling when tears form in her eyes.

He pulls out and she gasps in a breath, just for it to get cut off by him thrusting into her mouth again. "Fuck, sweetheart. You take my cock down your pretty little throat so well."

She whimpers as he finds a pace, keeping his thrusts shallow so she gets a little break. I keep an eye on her hands.

You can do anything to me. I trust you.

That's not a trust I plan on breaking. Fucking ever.

When Rhett forces Wren to take all of his dick again, she chokes. Tears fall onto her cheeks, wetting the mascara and causing it to run.

"You look fucking beautiful like this, sweetheart. My beautiful slut."

She moans, panting when he pulls out again. Drool coats her chin, and she wears it proudly, her eyes gleaming.

"You like choking on my cock, don't you?"

With a nod, she opens her mouth and sticks her tongue out, silently asking for more. He doesn't hesitate, fucking her mouth harder than before. As she takes it, she tries not to gag, but she can't help it.

Rhett doesn't stop until her face is soaked, covered in black streaks.

"So perfect," he says, dropping to his knees and holding her face in his hands. "I never want to forget the way you look right now."

The expression on her face is so satisfied, so content, you'd think she just came down from an orgasm.

"Thank you, Rhett."

"Oh, sweetheart. It was my goddamned pleasure." Grabbing his shirt from the floor, he uses it to wipe the drool from her mouth and chin. He leaves the tears and mascara, though. "Do you need more water?"

"Yes. But let Elliot get it. It's Oliver's turn with you."

For a second, he just stares at her in amazement that she understands. That she's so willing to share. And honestly, I think it's how we all feel—about how understanding she's been with *everything*.

After a long, slow kiss, Rhett stands. Oliver watches him, arms crossed, relaxed and still leaning against the dresser. Before Rhett all but mauls him, I grab the water glass from behind Oliver.

When I bring it to Wren's lips, she moans in appreciation, gulping it down. I pull it away from her lips before she takes too much.

"Easy. I think you've probably done enough choking for one night."

She giggles, and then I let her drain the glass, careful not to give her too much water at once. When I pull her up, her legs are a little wobbly, so I help her to the bed.

Her mouth opens in a silent laugh, her gaze fixated behind me. When I turn, I can't help but smile.

Oliver's legs are wrapped around Rhett's waist, who has him pressed against the wall beside my dresser. One of Rhett's hands is holding Oliver's ass, and the other has his wrists pinned to the wall above his head.

And . . . yeah. I don't even know if you could call what Rhett is doing to Oliver's mouth a kiss. It's more like an act of domination, a battle for his fucking soul.

Except Oliver is barely fighting. No, he's enjoying it too much.

"Oh my god," Wren says.

I'm not sure what the exact reasons Rhett had for avoiding Oliver all week. Or why Oliver let him do it for this long. If I had to guess, Rhett was probably afraid he wouldn't be understanding enough if Oliver broke down again—or that he'd trigger the breakdown. Both have happened before.

Who knows? I'm just glad they resolved things before I was driven to locking them in a room together until they fixed it.

For a minute longer, we watch Oliver and Rhett. Then I get on my knees in between Wren's legs.

"Do you want more, love?"

She raises an eyebrow. "Are you in on this too, now? Seeing how many times I can come in one night?"

I smirk. "Why not?"

When I press a kiss to her inner thigh, she bites her lip against a moan, and her legs spread.

"I need you to use your words, love."

"I want more," she whispers.

"Good. Because tasting you is all I could think about while I was watching you dance with Oliver."

"You were watching?"

"You think Oliver would've left you alone if I hadn't been?"

Realization settles on her features—that we fucking mean it when we say we won't let a single thing happen to her. I stand, pushing her back onto the bed. She wiggles, her hands still tied behind her back, trying to get comfortable.

"Do you want me to untie you?"

"No. I—I like how it feels."

Figured you would.

Back on my knees, I give her clit a single lick. "Tell me if it starts to hurt too much."

Her answer is a moan, because I'm slipping two fingers into her, curling them against her g-spot. I have every intention of taking my time enjoying her, but I have no problem making her come a couple times while I do.

When my tongue circles her clit, she jumps, groaning. *Fuck.* Half of me wants to gag her, just because I know she'd like it—and so would I—but the noises she makes are so goddamned perfect. I love her screams too much to muffle them.

With my free hand, I reach up to brush the pad of my thumb over one of her pebbled nipples. I can barely reach, but her breath hitching makes it worth it. Then I suck on her clit, and she cries out, her back arching for a second before she collapses onto the mattress.

She's so sensitive and worked up, she comes so fast I think it surprises even her. I slow my fingers and lick her clit gently, but she still squirms against me.

"Elliot, I need you to stop. Please stop, please."

I do, pulling my fingers from her.

She relaxes, panting. "Just for a second. Let me recover."

"Of course, love." I kiss her thigh. "That was six, right?"

She moans. "I've lost count."

"It's six," Rhett says.

"Jesus fuck," Wren whispers. After a minute, she says, "I'm ready."

With a hum of appreciation, I dive back in. She yelps, so I lighten the touch of my tongue. My hand snakes back up her side to tweak her nipple, and I splay the other across her lower stomach, pressing down.

"Oh my god. Fuck, Elliot, *ohhhh.*"

I alternate between massaging her clit with my tongue and sucking it into my mouth. She tastes sweet, mixed with something salty, that—if I had to guess—I'd say is probably Oliver's cum leaking out of her.

"Elliot, it feels so good. You feel so . . . *fuck.*"

I groan into her, lapping her up. Ever since we revealed our plan to her and she just accepted it, accepted *us,* I've needed to bury myself in her. Lose myself in her.

It all feels too fast, I suppose. There are only a couple people we've ever trusted with our true feelings toward Ludo. And letting Wren in so quickly was a huge leap of faith to take.

But she didn't let us down. After Tuesday, I knew she wouldn't.

"Elliot," she cries. And then she's coming again, her screams more sob-like than anything else.

My tongue leaves her clit, instead stimulating the skin right next to it. It does exactly what I want it to, drawing out her orgasm until her body is trembling like a leaf.

Seven.

When I pull away, her eyes are closed, and I'd think she was asleep if she wasn't muttering, "Oh my god, oh my god, oh my god," under her breath.

She looks peaceful and sated. But it's disturbed when Rhett shoves Oliver onto the bed next to her. He's on his stomach, grinning at Wren, eyeliner smudged.

"Hi, princess."

"Hi," she breathes.

Oliver reaches out to touch her face, and when his fingers feather over her lips, she presses a kiss to them.

"Mine," Rhett snaps, snatching his hand away and pinning it to Oliver's back.

With a snicker, Oliver whispers, "He can get a bit possessive during sex. You'll probably want to remember that."

She giggles.

I grab the lube and hand it to Rhett without him even having to ask. He pulls Oliver up so his ass is in the air and starts prepping him.

Standing, I squeeze Wren's thigh. "How are your arms, love?"

"Good." Then her eyes widen as she notices that I'm hard again.

"I can stop if you need me to. It's not a problem at all."

"No, I want to keep going. For . . . a bit longer."

"You're sure?"

"Mmhmm."

Oliver groans into the mattress. Rhett is fucking him with his fingers while still pinning his wrists to his back.

"I'm going to take your ass again, love."

I grab the lube from Rhett, squirting some on my fingers. Then, gently, I stretch Wren again, wanting to make sure she's ready. Her tiny whimpers shoot straight to my dick. Still, I take my time, not wanting to rush this. Rhett does the same.

When I finally slide into Wren, I use my clean hand and slip two fingers into her vagina. She groans, clenching around me, and it's so goddamned *tight.*

"Is this what you wanted all night? Huh?" Rhett taunts. He has his dick just barely inside Oliver.

"Longer than that, and you know it," Oliver groans. "Don't tease me."

With a smirk, Rhett slides all the way in. "Fuck," he groans.

"Yes. Exactly. Fuck me. *Now.*"

"So bossy," Rhett complains, smacking Oliver's ass. But he listens, pulling out before thrusting back in.

"Look at us, Wren. Getting the shit fucked out of us, together." He winks at her, mischief sparking in his eyes. "I'd kiss you if I could reach you."

Rhett smacks his ass again, and Oliver's entire face lights up with laughter. "Focus on me or I'll stop."

"He won't," Oliver whispers.

He doesn't. But Oliver also shuts the hell up, which is probably best for his ass cheeks.

Wren moans when I go harder. I can't help it. The sight of Rhett fucking Oliver is too hot.

Rhett comes first, which is no surprise considering how long he fucked Wren's mouth for.

"Oliver," he grits out, grabbing onto his hips. As his thrusts die off, his eyes slide closed, and his head drops to his chest.

For a minute he stays like that, working to regain his composure. Oliver tries to look back at him, but he really can't with his head pressed into the mattress, so he watches Wren instead.

That is, until Rhett pulls out and flips Oliver onto his back. He's on him in a split second, kissing Oliver like he'll die if he doesn't. Then, standing, he grabs Oliver's legs and yanks him to the edge of the bed.

As Rhett lowers himself to his knees, I freeze. It's not often that he puts himself in this position, kneeling for someone. It's too vulnerable for him, reminds him too much of things he'd prefer to never remember.

The same thoughts must be going through Oliver's head, because he's sitting up and shaking his head. "You don't have to—"

Rhett cuts him a sharp look. "Do you want to finish or not?"

That shuts Oliver right up. His eyes roll into the back of his head when Rhett fists the base of his cock, licking it before taking it into his mouth.

I groan at the sight. And then I remember that I'm still inside of Wren. When I turn, she's smiling up at me patiently, probably grateful for the chance to catch her breath.

I pick up my pace again, pressing my fingers into her walls as well. Her breasts bounce every time I slam into her, and her eyes turn foggy. She's drowning in the sensations, in the emotions, in all of us.

When I press my thumb to her clit, she comes undone almost immediately. Her back arches as her hips jerk, trying to find relief from my touch.

"Too sensitive," she cries.

I pull my hand away, and she groans in relief, sagging into the bed. She's well and truly used up and limp, just like Rhett promised she would be.

"Eight," I say, but I'm not sure she hears me.

From there, it doesn't take long before I come again. It hits me so hard that all I want to do is collapse onto the bed on the other side of Wren. But I need to get her out of the ropes first. So after I give myself enough time that I can see straight again, I sit on the bed, pulling her up.

When her hands are free, she rolls her shoulders and wrists, beaming at me. "Thank you."

"Of course, love." I kiss her lightly.

"Fuck. *Fuck,* Rhett." Oliver throws his head back as he finishes in Rhett's mouth, gripping the blankets. Rhett swallows every drop of cum Oliver gives him, licking his lips when he's done. Before he stands, he presses a kiss to Oliver's thigh.

The four of us look at each other, breathless and dazed. That was… well, I think Wren sums it up the best when she says, "Holy fuck."

Oliver snickers. "If you think a single thing we just did was holy, we did something wrong."

She's too tired to laugh, but she smiles. "If it sends me to hell, I'll go gladly."

Chapter Seventeen

Oliver

After we say goodnight, Elliot takes Wren into his shower, and I drag Rhett into mine. He washes me silently. Tenderly. I don't know how he's managing this much vulnerability without getting all tense and awkward, but I don't care. I'm just grateful we're back to being okay.

"Are you going to be able to sleep?" I ask as we dry off.

"I think so. You all wore me out."

After hanging up my towel, I start to leave the bathroom, but he grabs my arm. His towel is knotted around his waist.

"Wait." He tugs me over to the counter, and when he picks up the orange prescription pill bottle, my stomach turns.

"Rhett—"

"Elliot counted the pills and did the math. You stopped taking them a week ago."

"I . . ."

Unscrewing the cap, he shakes a pill into his palm. "We'll talk about it later. But for now—" He doesn't have to finish, holding his hand out to me instead.

I take the pill, swallowing it dry. "I'm sorry."

He shakes his head. "You're not less of a person because you have to take them, O."

My shoulders sag as he pulls me close.

"Thank you for tonight," he murmurs, kissing my forehead.

It eases the ache in my chest. When he pulls away, I grin. "I think Wren and I should jump you more often."

He snorts. "Maybe we'll jump you."

"You say it like I wouldn't be okay with that."

Rolling his eyes, he shoves me toward my room. "Bed. Now."

I bury myself under my covers, watching Rhett as he finishes getting ready for bed. When he climbs under the blankets, he doesn't pull me into his arms. I wish he would, but I understand why he needs his space.

I take in his face before he shuts off the lamp. He looks as happy as I feel—which for Rhett means there's the barest hint of a smile on his lips.

It doesn't take long before I'm drifting off into a light sleep. My breathing must deepen, because the words that come out of Rhett's mouth aren't ones he'd say if he thought I was still awake.

He shows it—all the fucking time. Every single day. But he rarely ever *says* it.

"I know you know," he says quietly. "And I know you don't mind that I don't say it often. But I love you, Oliver."

I don't reply, don't react, too scared to make him uncomfortable. I have to blink back the tears filling my eyes at the same time that I smile into the darkness.

I love you, too, Rhett.

Chapter Eighteen

Wren

After we shower, Elliot pulls me into a hot bath, saying something about not wanting me to be too sore tomorrow. I'm exhausted and all I want to do is sleep, but that also means I'm too tired to protest.

Elliot helps me into the tub, and I sink into the water in between his legs. It reminds me so much of the first couple of nights I spent with them, barely even a week ago.

Jesus Christ. It's only been a week?

So much has happened. I've settled into the feeling of fitting with Elliot, Rhett, and Oliver. Tuesday certainly flipped everything around, but it's not like I didn't know what I was getting myself into. *Somewhat.* They told me their lifestyle was dangerous. So I wasn't too surprised when I got pulled into it.

It was still a lot to handle at once, though. And I *definitely* didn't expect that one of their main goals in life is to tear apart a certain man's life.

But that certain man happens to deserve it.

My heart squeezes when I remember the pain in Rhett's eyes at the club. Finding out that Holloway killed Sammy, having to watch him relive the agony of losing her, it was heartbreaking.

Elliot strokes his fingers down my arm, and I moan, too tired to try and make conversation.

He lets out a low, amused sound. "You're falling asleep again, aren't you?"

"No," I say, my eyelids drooping. "But if I was, it's your fault." I yawn. "You fucked all the energy right out of me."

He presses a kiss to my hair, and I settle against him. So warm. So comforting. So . . . *yes*.

My feelings for these men keep growing, stretching into an endless abyss that I'm tumbling further and further into.

The thing is, I realize as I begin to fall asleep with my head on Elliot's chest, I don't think I ever want to stop falling.

To be continued . . .

Deleted Scene

If you want to read one of the deleted scenes from Perfect Convergence, go to subscribepage.io/pc-bonus and sign up to my email list.

Author's Note

Thanks so much for reading Perfect Convergence! It was so much fun writing the sequel to Blissful Masquerade, and I hope you enjoyed it. The story will continue in Ruthless Desires #3.

I've been writing since I was a teenager. Creating different storyworlds and characters was my absolute favorite pastime (okay, okay, coping mechanism). I've always loved romance, especially dark romance with a little suspense sprinkled in, so it's no surprise that it's what I ended up writing.

If you'd like to stay up to date with my latest writings and adventures, you can check out my website elirafirethorn.com or follow me on Instagram, Pinterest, and TikTok @elirafirethorn.

Also By Elira Firethorn

Dark Luxuries Trilogy
Deepest Obsession
Twisted Redemption
Darkest Retribution

Ruthless Desires Series
Blissful Masquerade
Perfect Convergence

Printed in Great Britain
by Amazon